SAVING KATIE

BROTHERHOOD PROTECTORS WORLD

TENNESSEE TASK FORCE
BOOK TWO

KAREN HALL

Twisted Page Press LLC

BROTHERHOOD PROTECTORS

ORIGINAL SERIES BY ELLE JAMES

Brotherhood Protectors Colorado World
Team Watchdog
Mason's Watch - Jen Talty
Asher's Watch - Leanne Tyler
Cruz's Watch - Stacey Wilk
Kent's Watch- Deanna L. Rowley
Ryder's Watch- Kris Norris

Team Eagle
Booker's Mission - Kris Norris
Hunter's Mission - Kendall Talbot
Gunn's Mission - Delilah Devlin
Xavier's Mission - Lori Matthews
Wyatt's Mission - Jen Talty

Team Raptor
Darius' Promise - Jen Talty
Simon's Promise - Leanne Tyler
Nash's Promise - Stacey Wilk
Spencer's Promise - Deanna L. Rowley
Logan's Promise - Kris Norris

Team Falco

Fighting for Esme - Jen Talty
Fighting for Charli - Leanne Tyler
Fighting for Tessa - Stacey Wilk
Fighting for Kora - Deanna L. Rowley
Fighting for Fiona - Kris Norris

Athena Project
Beck's Six - Desiree Holt
Victoria's Six - Delilah Devlin
Cygny's Six - Reina Torres
Fay's Six - Jen Talty
Melody's Six - Regan Black

Team Trojan
Defending Sophie - Desiree Holt
Defending Evangeline - Delilah Devlin
Defending Casey - Reina Torres
Defending Sparrow - Jen Talty
Defending Avery - Regan Black

Brotherhood Protectors Yellowstone World
Team Wolf
Guarding Harper - Desiree Holt
Guarding Hannah - Delilah Devlin
Guarding Eris - Reina Torres
Guarding Payton - Jen Talty
Guarding Leah - Regan Black

CHAPTER 1

Present day, *Knoxville, Tennessee*
Monday morning

"I think I've been made, Annie." The long-haired and matted bearded man on the bench beside her drummed trembling fingers on the knees of his ripped jeans. His gaze darted around the square, studying the faces of the passers-by while shifting his weight from side to side, his battered shoes beating a rapid tattoo on the sidewalk.

Beneath her suit jacket, Anne Hamilton shivered. He seldom called her Annie and it set off every warning signal she'd developed in her nine years as a reporter. The late October afternoon was glorious as the autumn light faded, while shoppers exited the stores and boutiques with oversized bags and brightly wrapped packages, kicking their way through the russet and yellow leaves carpeting the sidewalks.

But Anne knew with an unfailing certainty that the man beside her was nervous, and a rare apprehension shuttled over her skin. If he was nervous, then something was very wrong. "Made?" Her own hands were not quite steady as she put the food bag between them. "By whom? No one's ever guessed who you are before. What's happened?"

"Weird things," he answered, taking a sandwich from the bag and devouring it. "Over the last few months, most of my snitches have stopped talking to me, and last week the guys I've played penny poker with for years are refusing to meet with me."

"How could they have figured out who you are?" Anne kept her gaze on the plate glass window of a nearby restaurant. For the past five years, this man, known to her as Henry Cooper, a confidential informant for the police, had sometimes shared information about street crime she'd have never found on her own after he'd told the police. He was a CI for many years standing. After reading one of Anne's stories in her newspaper *Excelsior*, he'd asked his police contact to introduce them. They'd developed a professional but guarded relationship and she knew to wait for him to reach out to her.

But it had been eight months since she'd heard from him and the difference in his appearance alarmed her. While he used a variety of disguises, she would have known him from his cobalt blue eyes. And he'd always been reasonably well groomed, his hair and beard trimmed, clothes neat and clean. Not like this.

"Don't know," he admitted, licking his fingers and wiping them on his jeans. "But my only snitch who's still talking to me confirmed yesterday what I've suspected since May. The Cadre moved into the area six months ago. I think they may have snatched Katie Johnson and those other missing kids."

Horror-laced dread drenched Anne's skin. Katie Johnson was her best friend Clare's only daughter and Anne's "niece." Five days ago, she'd boarded her school bus at the end of the day, reportedly got off at her usual stop but never came home. She was the sixth high school student who had simply "vanished" in the past three weeks. None of the parents had received word from or of them, leaving them in a nightmare hell of panic and fear. Despite their best efforts, the police had found nothing, and the community was in an uproar, demanding something be done. School attendance had dropped.

The Cadre, a crime organization out of Chicago, was known for moving into other areas and seizing power from local crime groups by any means necessary. They were also one of the biggest traffickers of teens in the country, preying on street kids and runaways but often snatching other kids off the streets.

"If The Cadre has been here for six months, then why did your snitch wait so long to tell you?" Anne choked back the bile rising in her throat. Bright, pretty, dog-loving Katie in the hands of The Cadre? She'd be terrified.

"Because The Cadre always 'lays low and starts slow' when they move into a new area," Henry rasped. "That way, it's a long time before the police know it's them. That's how they got the nickname Los Silenciosos. 'Silent Ones'. And my snitch is so damn scared of them he's been hiding for weeks 'cause he thinks *he's* been made. Everyone is scared. Hell, I'm scared of them. Why do you think I look like this? I've been even more undercover, trying to find out if it was them for months."

Pushing down her rising panic, Anne forced her reporter's brain into working mode. "Do the police know they're here?"

Beneath the smudge-stained face, Henry's sudden smile held all his old cockiness. "Yeah, they do because I told them. They've suspected something was going on, but their other CIs are so scared, they ain't talking either, so the information flow between 'em has dried up. No one is talking to anyone."

"I'm glad you're still talking to me," Anne said.

"Have the police told Katie's parents The Cadre might have her?"

"No, and you're not going to tell them or the others either because we don't know they've got them," Henry ordered. "But my snitch did say the street word is The Cadre is getting ready to transport a bunch of local teens to bigger places any day now. And Annie, The Cadre probably knows you wrote that story last year that all but accused them of being responsible for all those kids from Gainesville 'vanishing', even if you used a pseudonym. That may be another reason why they've come here."

The uncharacteristic wobble in his voice sent a fresh wave of fear sweeping over her and Anne realized he wasn't just afraid for himself but for her as well. Mouth dry, she folded her hands together so he wouldn't see them trembling. "You mean I've been made as well?"

His silence told her all she needed to know. For the first time since he sat down, she openly stared at him. His ripped jeans showed that his knees as well as his palms were badly scraped. Beneath the filth, his face was bruised, and his fingers swollen. "Did someone hurt you?"

"Yesterday a guy shoved me into a building and on the way here, another tripped me. I found this on the sidewalk when I stood." He fished a paper scrap from his jeans pocket and held it out. A printed message warned, "**MiNd Ure OwN dam bizzness**."

"You have been made," she whispered, shoving the scrap into her jacket pocket. "What do we do now?"

"Right now, I'm walking you to your car and you're going back to the paper and talking to your editor." Henry tossed the food bag into a nearby trash can. "He needs to know what's going on in case..." He did not have to finish his sentence. If The Cadre had "made" them. . . Anne shoved the thought away. Henry was right. She needed to get back to the paper.

They stood and it was his turn to stare at her. "Why are you so dressed up? Suit, heels, and stockings?"

"I had a meeting at the mayor's office before I came here," she said. She always wore jeans, sweat-shirts, and no makeup when they met, so no one would recognize her. She never let her photo be used in her articles, but as Henry often said, "the streets have eyes and ears" and her writing was well-known enough locally that many knew who she was. Today her attire marked her as someone other than one of Henry's buddies.

The walk to her old RAV-4 was a short one, but the remaining daylight was fading fast, and she began to scan the faces of the people they passed. Behind her, the slap of Henry's battered soles on the pavement should have brought her some comfort, but her pulse was pounding with a skin-bruising force. They'd almost reached her car when Henry said, "Hold up a minute."

Reaching into his jeans pocket, he pulled out two keys on a metal ring and gave them to her. "These are to the place I'm staying, just in case."

"Just in case of what?" she asked as they stepped off the curb.

The screech of rushing tires was followed by screaming voices to *Move! Get out of the way!* as Henry's hard body tackled hers, knocking her through the air. She hit the sidewalk, her hands and knees sliding along the surface, tearing her stockings as her fingers clawed, searching for some spot to grab and stop her movement.

Dazed, she raised and saw Henry's crumpled body before she collapsed back on the sidewalk.

Hours later, after refusing admission for overnight observation and the ER doctor had declared Henry Cooper dead, Anne let Stanley Harris, her editor at *Excelsior,* take her back to the office to call Brotherhood Protectors.

CHAPTER 2

Tuesday Afternoon/Ramsey's Hotel
  Knoxville, Tennessee

"Here's what we're up against, Mac." Brotherhood Protector's founder Hank Patterson's expression on the monitor's screen was grim. "First, the security system there at *Ramsey's* has been compromised, so we're moving to The Oasis, our new safe house south of town for now."

"That's a shame." Lt. Keith "Mac" MacFarlane, USMC, retired, leaned back into the comfort of the familiar office chair. Brotherhood Protectors had purchased the entire fifth floor of *Ramsey's* hotel in downtown Knoxville this past spring. With its state-of-the-art computer system, excellent restaurant, and luxurious rooms overlooking an area of the city known as Our Place, it made the very hard work BP often did easier. "What's our assignment?"

"Police informants have confirmed their suspicions that The Cadre arrived in Knoxville six months ago and–"

"Holy shit." Mac's stomach twisted into knots. "The Cadre is in Knoxville?"

"According to our police contacts," Hank confirmed. "Over the last three weeks, they're suspected of snatching six teens, one as recently as six days ago and are preparing to transport them to bigger cities where they've got buyers waiting. Since you're in Knoxville, and you've had training regarding The Cadre for work with Tennessee Task Force, you're the logical choice."

It's not your fault. The Sayyid children being killed was not your fault. The voice of Drew Carter, his VA therapist whispered in Mac's memory. He silently recited an old Gaelic prayer for strength and reviewed what he knew. The Cadre was a crime organization out of Chicago, notorious for moving into new areas and taking over the established gangs through violence and intimidation, doing it so quietly and without notice, that they'd earned the nickname, Los Silenciosos. Silent Ones.

They were also suspected of running one of the country's biggest networks for abducting kids and teens, trafficking and selling them to the highest bidders. The bile rose in Mac's throat and he poured cold water from the carafe on the desk into his oversized mug and took a long sip. "What are the particulars of the case?"

"Late yesterday afternoon, Henry Cooper, a CI in Knoxville, died in a hit-and-run accident," Hank began. "A local reporter, Anne Hamilton, was with him and slightly injured, but only because Cooper shoved her out of the way. Stanley Harris, her editor at *Excelsior,* knows about us and called after he picked Ms. Hamilton up from the ER and we three had a Zoom meeting. Since her only injuries were bruises, scrapes, and according to Harris, a shredded pair of pantyhose and a ruined manicure, she refused to stay overnight at the hospital. But Harris thinks someone was trying to kill her as well and will try again."

Mac frowned. "Why do we think The Cadre was behind this attack? And was the target Cooper or Ms. Hamilton?"

"The police think both," Hank shared. "Cooper was one of their CIs for years and if they cleared it, he's passed some of his information to Ms. Hamilton, who wrote about it. One of Cooper's sources told him a few days ago that The Cadre was in town, and he told the police."

"And Cooper told Ms. Hamilton, and someone ran over them, killing Cooper," Mac guessed. "Someone betrayed him, is that it?"

"Looks like," Hank answered. "Ms. Hamilton is lucky she wasn't killed."

"What's The Cadre's beef with her?" Mac asked. "Other than she worked with Cooper?"

"Do you remember that news story last year, 'Not in My Backyard' about child trafficking in Gainesville?" Hank asked. "That was Anne Hamilton's story. She practically accused The Cadre of being responsible and the story went viral, in print and online in almost every major newspaper in the country. She wrote under a pseudonym, but I have no doubt The Cadre knows exactly who wrote it."

"I read it," Mac said softly. Its account of exploited and trafficked some as young as five years old was precise and well researched, its prose style smooth and elegant in its simplicity but took no prisoners. "I'll bet The Cadre is pissed off. Is Tennessee Task Force involved in this?"

Tennessee Task Force, a new multi-agency program, including law enforcement, was designed to find and rescue exploited and missing children. The program was still being finalized but BP had offered its services if needed. Mac had helped with the case involving an endangered child last spring that started the Task Force, but he'd mostly stayed in the background. After some training with them, he'd accepted other assignments from Hank, taking him out of state. He'd returned to Knoxville last night after attending a retreat with fellow Marines this past weekend.

"Indirectly," Hank said. "But both the attacks on Cooper and Ms. Hamilton and the suspected abduction of the six teens are part of a criminal investigation, so unless asked, we're out of the loop. Our job is to protect Anne Hamilton."

"And of course, The Cadre has been doing business in their usual sneaky 'low and slow' MO," Mac added. "They move in without notice, lay low and before you know it, they're in control after convincing local gangs and crime groups to either give up their power and join them or face retaliation. What's the local crime scene since The Cadre arrived?"

"An upsurge in illegal gun sales, more drugs coming in, including a sharp increase in the amounts of opiate and fentanyl-related deaths." Anger laced Hank's voice, giving it an ominous edge. "That alone has kept the police busier than usual over the last six months. But now they know it's probably because of The Cadre."

"And since The Cadre scares the hell out of anyone and everyone who gets in their way, the street snitches keep it zipped," Mac added.

A slow burn inched up his spine but his nod for the local police was empathetic. He'd met several of them this past spring on the other BP case and they were the best of the best. "Is Ms. Hamilton involved with the missing teens?"

Hank's mouth tightened and he nodded. "Her adopted niece, Katie Johnson, was the last of the six to vanish. There's been no word from them or to their families from anyone, The Cadre or otherwise. According to Ms. Hamilton, Cooper suspected The Cadre had them, but he didn't have any details."

"And Ms. Hamilton is dead set on finding her niece and the other kids," Mac guessed. "Hence, her editor's call to us."

"That's it," Hank agreed. "My impression is she is one determined woman, even in the best of circumstances. If she thinks The Cadre has her niece, she's going to try to go after them."

"So, BP's mission is to protect Ms. Hamilton, hopefully, find Katie and the others while we do it, and take down those sons-of bitches," Mac declared. "Sounds like fun."

"Exactly," Hank said, and Mac recognized the fury smoldering in his boss's green eyes. There wasn't a single member of Brotherhood Protectors who wouldn't gladly go after the monsters and deviants who preyed on children. He chuckled at the thought of what Hank Patterson, proud papa of little Emma, would do to those bastards if *he* ever got his hands on even one of them.

"Now, before I send you Ms. Hamilton's contact

information, I want you to remember something," Hank said, leaning forward. "What happened to the five Sayyid children in Afghanistan was not your fault. You couldn't know those renegades would ride up on motorcycles and gun down almost everyone in the square."

"I should have made them go inside the café with me," Mac said woodenly. "But they wanted to stay outside and watch that old man do magic tricks while I bought them breakfast. They were always so hungry."

"And you said Ahmed was indignant that you thought he couldn't watch his younger sibs for a few minutes," Hank reminded him. "Since his father died, he was the 'man' of the family, even if he was only ten years old."

Mac allowed himself a smile. "He said, 'You go buy eggs, naan and tea, Big Dude. That's your job. I watch the kids. That's my job.'"

"And it could have happened to anyone in your unit," Hank continued. "You just happened to be the one walking them to school that day."

"But it did happen to me," Mac countered. Hank was the only one besides his therapist who knew he still struggled with inner demons over the Sayyid children's deaths. The thought of someone hurting kids always ignited a desire to stop those who did, no matter what. As an uncle several times over, Mac had lots of practice with young kids.

Not my fault. Mac had told himself that a thousand times. But at times the guilt would roar back, leaving a searing hurt and a choking anger.

But he had to get past it. He was toast if he didn't.

"Your actual contact with kids will be minimal if any," Hank said, as if reading his mind. "Your primary job will be to keep Ms. Hamilton safe while the police look for The Cadre. As a reporter, she's gonna be gung-ho to find out who killed her friend and who has her niece and the others. Use that Scottish charm of yours to keep her on a leash. Her boss called me privately and said she's as stubborn as they come and will probably do what she wants. Are you up for this?"

Sweat broke out on Mac's forehead. Hank Patterson's regard meant almost as much as his parents' good opinion. Memories of the laughing Sayyid children danced before his eyes and for a moment, he couldn't speak.

But then Mac remembered who he was. Lt. Keith MacFarlane, USMC and proud member of the Brotherhood Protectors. He met Hank's gaze. "On it," he said, hauling out his confidence. "What do you want me to do first?"

"Get in touch with Anne Hamilton," Hank directed. "I'm forwarding her information. She already has yours. Harris told her–ordered her is how I think he phrased it–to take off the rest of the week, but he has his doubts. Be safe, Mac."

His screen image faded, and Mac opened Anne Hamilton's file. He stared at the reporter's photo and released an appreciative sigh. Jade green eyes fixed the viewer with a cool confidence and her shoulder-length black hair gleamed like polished onyx. Gold spirals glittered from her ears, and her open-necked blouse hinted at marvels beneath it.

But it was her mouth that got him. Full, lush, and red. He could envision kissing it for hours and wondered how it would taste.

Then he shook himself. Between her refined appearance and fussing about her ripped pantyhose and ruined manicure, Anne Hamilton was too high maintenance for him. Mac preferred his women down to earth. He profoundly hoped she realized just how much danger she was in. With Henry Cooper dead, six missing kids, and The Cadre after her, there was no time to waste. He would protect Anne Hamilton and find the missing kids while he did it. Failure was not an option. He had to succeed. He owed it to the Sayyid kids. He owed it to these missing kids. And he owed it to himself.

"I'll find them," he whispered, offering up the words as a promise and a prayer. "I'll find them."

CHAPTER 3

"You've been made too. Henry's unspoken words drummed in Anne's memory as she started her car and backed out of the garage. She still couldn't wrap her head around the fact that he was dead and realized, not for the first time, how little she knew about him. Knew him.

She knew he liked Thai food, loaded hot dogs, and red velvet cake. He was a rabid follower of the Lady Vols Basketball Team and the Tennessee Titans and he was sometimes seen at Morning Prayer at the Episcopal Cathedral downtown.

But where he'd come from, and how he'd ended up as a CI? She didn't even know where he'd lived. After all this time, she should have known that. The information he'd fed her over the years–which she always gave the police in case he couldn't get to them–had often been the key to solving cases. He'd been helpful, funny, and kind. And why had he given her the keys to his place?

Now he was dead, killed saving her life. Tears stung her eyes, and she blinked them back. It was not a comfortable feeling.

At least her grandmother's "magic cream" had taken the sting out of her scraped knees and palms. Anne was still trying to get her to divulge the recipe for it. Several long soaks with her favorite bath salts had eased most of the aches from her muscles so walking was not quite as painful. And vain as it was, her new mani-pedi just made her feel, if not look, better. Sometimes a girl just had to do these things.

But since the accident, her sleep was almost non-existent. Between her constant worry over Katie, combined with thoughts and dreams of the accident that killed Henry–the bystander's screams, the screeching of the tires and her hitting the pavement after he shoved her away–had kept her mostly awake the past two nights. The sky was swollen and overcast, with gray clouds threatening rain, matching her mood.

Her phone buzzed from its holder on the dash, and she recognized the number as the one Hank Patterson had sent for her Brotherhood Protectors contact. She hit the phone's accept button and said, "Lt. MacFarlane?"

"Ms. Anne Hamilton?" A voice with just a hint of a Scottish burr answered.

"Yes," she acknowledged. "Are you at the church? Or do you need directions? Do you have GPS in your car or on your phone?" They'd chosen to meet at the Church of The Living Water in East Knoxville. Most people had GPS in their cars or on their phones, but others, like her friend Lucy, whose car and phone had every bell and whistle imaginable, still managed to get lost regularly, so Anne always asked.

But surely not a former Marine. He'd have both.

"I'm already there," MacFarlane said. "I heard the breakfast they offer on Wednesdays is very good. Want me to save you some ham and biscuits? Or would you rather have sausage?"

"Just as long as they still have coffee," she replied, backing out of the garage and closing it with the remote. "You said you'd be driving a black Dodge Ram truck. Lots of people around here drive those. How will I recognize you? For some reason, your photo didn't come through with your phone number."

His answering chuckle was deep and kind of sexy. "I don't think you'll have trouble spotting me, Ms. Hamilton. I'm what they call a tall drink of water."

Great. My CI is rundown and killed and I am being forced to work with some guy who thinks he's a comedian. "Really," she managed to say.

"Really," he agreed. "Are you en route?"

"I'm on the way," she acknowledged, pulling onto her street. "Hanging up to drive now."

"I'm parked in the back," he said. "Be safe."

The drive to the church was not far, but Anne took her time, reflecting on what Stanley Harris had told her about Brotherhood Protectors after the Zoom meeting. BP, as they were sometimes called, was a rather formidable sounding group of veterans– men and women who now used their skills to provide help and protection to those in need of it, which was why Stanley had called them. Lt. MacFarlane was a part of BP.

She wasn't sure she needed or wanted any protection, but Harris wouldn't budge on that point. "You'll take it if you want to help find out who killed Henry," he'd told her when she'd gone to the office yesterday to convince him otherwise. "No discussion, Anne. And as far as the staff knows, what happened to Henry was an accident. No need to tell them it's not only an active homicide investigation, but an attempted one as well. They're already freaking out about this."

An attempted homicide of *her*. Shivering, she turned up the heat. She'd been cold ever since the accident and was glad she'd chosen her favorite long-sleeve dress that matched her eyes and a black cardigan-style jacket to put her in a professional mood.

She pulled into the church's back parking lot and found a space far enough from the back doors that would allow her enough time to walk and switch on her journalist persona. Volunteers were placing paper grocery bags on tables under a large awning or helping carry the bags to cars.

Getting out of the RAV, her gaze was immediately directed to one of the tallest men she'd ever seen, leaning against a black 4-door Dodge Ram truck. His thick auburn hair almost touched his coat's collar, just begging for her fingers to explore it, and his beard was neatly trimmed. His heavy jacket clung to a set of powerful shoulders and his legs seemed to go on forever. Incredibly, her heart beat a little faster and she had to remind herself to keep focused. A tall drink of water indeed.

His gaze met hers and a smile lit up his face, making him even more handsome. He moved forward with a long, easy gait until they were facing each other. He cocked his head to look down at her, and for a moment she wished that despite her ankles still hurting just a bit, she'd worn her boots. In her one-inch heels, she barely came up to his shoulders. "Anne Hamilton?" he asked.

"Lt. Keith MacFarlane?" She took his offered hand.

"They call me 'Mac,'" he said. His eyes twinkled, and his grin was a toe-curling thing. "I see you got a manicure. Did you get your toes done too?"

She tilted her head back to stare at him. "I beg your pardon?"

"Nothing," he said, waving away the comment. "Let's go inside and get you that coffee. Have you had breakfast?"

"No," she admitted, falling into step beside him. "I overslept and hardly had time to shower before coming here."

"Well then, we must get ye fed." The faint Scottish accent she'd heard returned, but thicker. "A wee lassie like yourself needs to keep up her strength."

Her lack of sleep since the accident almost made Anne forget her manners-professional and otherwise. "You're very sure of yourself," she said tersely. "Is that the Marine in you?"

"Aye." His smile vanished and his eyes were an amazing shade of copper darkened to bronze. A volunteer opened the door for them, and they stepped into a vestibule of a large room. "And from what I've heard, you've not had an easy time of it over the past few days." He made a slight bow and gestured for her to enter first. "After you," he said.

Inside, the room was packed. To one side was a long row of tables loaded with steam trays. A tall, African American man in a clerical collar and an apron embroidered with the name and logo of the church, stood behind them, flanked by others wearing the same aprons who were busy serving eggs, bacon, sausage, ham, biscuits, and gravy and pancakes. Other volunteers moved around offering refills of beverages or clearing tables. The lit candles, cloth napkins, and heavy tablecloths gave the room a homey, welcoming fill.

As they approached, the pastor raised his arm and called, "Hey, Anne! Come have breakfast!"

"Hey, Pastor Cole," she called back. "I'd love some."

Her companion peered down at her, and she could almost feel the annoyance rolling off him. "You didn't tell me you know the staff here," he murmured.

"You didn't ask," she whispered back.

They stopped at the steam tables and Anne said, "Pastor Thomas Cole, meet Lt. Keith MacFarlane, USMC, retired. He's helping me with a story. Lt. MacFarlane, this is Pastor Thomas Cole, senior pastor of The Church of the Living Waters."

The men shook hands and after they'd filled their plates and cups-Anne taking only a sausage biscuit and coffee-Pastor Cole led them to a table on the far side of the room. When they were seated, he said, "I read about your accident, Anne. I'm very grateful you weren't hurt. And I'm sorry about your friend being killed. Do the police have any leads?"

"Not yet," she said after savoring a bite of the sausage biscuit, followed by a long swallow of coffee. "Pastor Cole, what have you heard about the rise in crime in Knoxville in the last six months or so? Has there been any in the surrounding neighborhood? Or talk of teens gone missing?"

Cole propped his elbows on the table and folded his hands together. "There's been a rise in the homeless population," he said slowly. "Folks from outside hear there's more help to be had here than in some of the rural communities, so they come looking for it. And there has been a rise in crime since the beginning of the year, but not necessarily in the neighborhood surrounding our church. And I don't think the homeless have anything to do with that. They're too busy trying to survive. Are you doing a story about that?"

Anne hesitated. "Maybe," she admitted. "Any talk of any other missing kids?"

"Other than the recent six?" Cole asked. "Not that I've heard. My congregation is very worried about their own kids' safety."

He hesitated and lowered his voice. "There's talk of some group coming here several months ago from Chicago, looking for street kids to exploit. They claim to offer them opportunities to start over as dancers, models, and stuff like that, but that's a bunch of crap. Word is that these are some very scary people who want the kids for other reasons. We've warned our youth to steer clear of anyone making that kind of offer and to tell their parents and me immediately."

"The Cadre?" Ms. Hamilton asked softly, and Cole nodded. No surprise, Mac thought, that a pastor of a community church that served those that the rest of the community too often over-looked would have heard talk about any threat to those he served. Especially a threat like The Cadre.

But to mention The Cadre to Pastor Cole by name?

"Are you thinking they might have taken your niece and those other kids?" Cole asked, folding his hands together.

Mac watched Ms. Hamilton push aside her plate with its half-finished biscuit and reach for her coffee. Her complexion was pale, her features so tightly drawn that even the skin under her eyes looked tired and he wondered how much she'd slept over the past few days.

"Maybe," she said at last. "Do you know anyone familiar with the streets I can talk to about the missing kids? They're not from the street but maybe that person has heard something the police haven't. Katie's family hasn't heard anything from her or about her and they're sick with worry."

"I'll bet they are," Cole agreed softly. His eyes narrowed

in thought. "There may be someone, but I'll

have to ask," he finally said. "I have your phone number, so I'll text you when I know something. Give me a day or two."

"Thanks, Pastor." Her hands were not quite steady as she lowered her cup to the table and Mac fought the urge to cover them with his own. He traded glances with Cole who gave a near-invisible shake of his head. He'd noticed too.

"Anne's a big asset to the church," Cole said now. "Helps cook the yearly Thanksgiving community dinner, gets local businesses to contribute to the Christmas toy drive, and helps get folks registered to vote. She's one of our best volunteers."

"Really?" Tamping down his surprise, Mac watched the 'volunteer' finish her coffee. "Member here, is she?"

"For a long time," Pastor Cole affirmed. "When she was still at UT, Anne was the one who started the program for graduate students to come three times a week and offer counseling and tutoring for anyone who needed it. This church serves as many families as we can and it can feel overwhelming at times, but we keep on keepin' on."

"Thanks, Pastor Cole," Anne said as they all stood. "I appreciate your willingness to help."

"We're all part of God's community," Cole said. "I'll keep you, the Johnsons, and the other families in my prayers. Oops, my wife is waving at me. Guess I better get back to work."

He moved away and they headed to the door, the soft click of her heels striking against the linoleum. They exited the building to step into a misting rain and Mac said, "You didn't mention this was your church. You might have told me if only for courtesy's sake. And do you think it was wise to tell Cole about The Cadre?"

"You didn't ask," she retorted. "Didn't your boss give you a copy of my life history or is he too busy saving the world? This is Pastor Cole's community. He needs to know if his congregation is in danger. He'd heard about The Cadre, if not by name, so I wasn't going to deny it. Pastors aren't stupid, you know."

An unfamiliar irritation at her abruptness flashed over Mac and he fought the desire to shake her. "Look, Ms. Hamilton," he said, biting off his words as they stopped serval hundred feet from her car. "Brotherhood Protectors is here at your employer's request because he thought you needed us. If you don't want our services, take it up with him. Someone killed your CI and nearly killed you. From where I stand, you're the next target. So why don't you drop the attitude and–"

The ear-splitting blast shattered the quiet as her car exploded. Mac seized her and pulled them both to the ground, covering her with his body as broken glass and twisted metal showered down on them. Black plumes billowed from her parking spot, polluting the air with a nose-burning stench as flames consumed what was left of the RAV-4. Beneath him, he felt her heart's frantic rhythm and heard her struggle to bring her choked, labored breathing under control as he blinked through the eye-searing, acrid smoke. From behind him, he could hear shouts and cries and the sound of running feet.

Slowly he rolled over and she did the same. Together they watched columns of billowing smoke rise into the October sky, listening to the wailing sirens' approach.

"Yeah," Mac finally said. "You need Brotherhood Protectors."

CHAPTER 4

Later that afternoon

"Very sophisticated style of bombs that can be started remotely," Daniel Tucker, KPD's bomb expert announced, matter-of-factly. He might have been describing the weather. "Small but very effective in blowing up things. You're damn lucky, Ms. Hamilton, that you weren't inside your car when it exploded."

"Thank you," Anne said automatically. Beside her, a grim-faced Lt. MacFarlane drummed his fingers on the table in Interview Room Number Three at the downtown police precinct. She tried to grab one of her spinning thoughts and slow it down long enough to form a question. "Was anyone hurt?"

"No, and no one else's vehicle was damaged," Tucker confirmed. "Good thing you parked so far in the back. But lots of people at the church are scared. Doc, are these two going to be okay?"

Andrea Riggs, MD, who'd come by the police station to bring her husband lunch had been pressed into service, nodded. "Just scrapes from where they hit the pavement," she said. "But I think it's safe to say they'll both live and be ready for work tomorrow."

"Thank you, Doctor Riggs," Lt. MacFarlane called as Tucker walked the tiny, older woman from the room. "How are you doing, Ms. Hamilton?"

Anne turned her gaze from the door to stare at MacFarlane. "They blew up my car," she said, as if saying it out loud might make it more believable. Because despite all the evidence, she was having a very hard time believing it. "They blew up my car."

"Yeah, they did," he replied. He frowned and something like concern shone in his eyes. "Are you sure you're alright?"

"I'm fine," Anne said, getting to her feet. "I should go apologize to Pastor Cole. What a terrible thing to happen at our church. I never should have suggested that we meet there. Is there someone who can drive–"

"You are not going anywhere," Lt. MacFarlane interrupted his strong hands gently but firmly pulling her back into the chair. Smoke residue had smudged his face, giving him the look of a very dangerous and very attractive man. "At least not anywhere near the church."

"Lt. MacFarlane is right," Tucker agreed, rejoining them. "It's a crime scene, so we're still asking questions of everyone who was at the church this morning. And you don't need to go back there in case whoever planted that bomb goes back."

Anne blinked. "Why would they go back?"

"Because when they realize you weren't in the car—"

"They're going to want to finish what they started," Anne completed. "Then what do we do?" She stared at the men, trying to pull her brain back into working mode. Exhaustion was making her feel stupid.

"We're going to let Tucker's people do their jobs," MacFarlane announced, and his lofty tone accelerated the impatience shimmying over Anne's skin. "Officer Tucker, when do I get my truck back? You said the bomb squad had gone over it and sent you a text saying they hadn't found anything."

"I'll go ask," Tucker offered. "Give me a minute."

He left, leaving the door half open and Anne fought the urge to slump over the table and go to sleep. Instead, she pulled out what strength she had in reserve to level her steeliest gaze at the man beside her. "Do you always take charge of a situation, Lieutenant?"

"When necessary, yeah." His eyes glittered with what Anne guessed was irritation, but his neutral expression gave away nothing of what he might be feeling or thinking. "And it's Mac. Since we're going to be spending a lot of time together, I'm hoping you'll let me call you Anne. Or is that going to be a problem?"

"Hey, Lt. MacFarlane." Tucker returned, pushing the door open. "Do you know this guy?"

"What's happening, Scotty?" A tall, grinning man with dark blond hair slipped past Tucker and pulled a now-standing Mac into a thumping hug. He was almost as handsome as "Scotty" and Anne wondered if belonging to BP required good looks.

"Tyler, you son-of-a sea serpent!" Mac shouted, returning the man's embrace. "When did you get into town?"

"Just now," the man said. "Got into Ashville late yesterday for some hiking but Hank called me a while ago and told me to get my ass over here because someone tried to blow you up."

"Something like," Mac agreed. There was no question as to what the Marine was feeling now. Any irritation towards Anne had vanished by the appearance of this other man, replacing it with shared feelings of men who have worked and fought together, and trusted each other. "We were about to go get my truck," he said.

"You're forgetting your manners, Scotty," the man teased. "Who is the beautiful lady sitting here giving you the devil's stare with those big green eyes?"

"I'm Anne Hamilton," she replied. "Why do you keep calling him 'Scotty'?"

"Because it usually pisses him off," the man laughed. "See that frown? I'm Griffin Tyler, and like this dunderhead here, "I'm retired USMC and now a BP member. My friends call me Griff."

"Happy to meet you, Griff," Anne said, thoroughly enjoying Mac's frown. "I'll remember the 'Scotty' thing."

"OK, that's enough chatter," Mac warned, but his smile was back. "Let's go get my truck."

"I'm your wheels." Griff gestured at Tucker. "His boss just told him your truck is still part of the crime scene, so it stays put for now."

"I promise we'll have it here first thing tomorrow," Tucker said, spreading his hands. "We'll have someone watch it until the scene is cleared and we bring it in. Sorry."

"Right," Mac said with the heartfelt sigh of a man who loves his truck.

After thanking Tucker again, Anne let Griff lead the way out of the room. Mac fell into step beside her so that she walked between them, listening to their banter, again marking them as 'brothers' in the best sense of the word. Outside, they reached a non-descript black sedan, obviously a rental, and once they were in the back seat, Griff said, "Hank brought me up to speed on the particulars of your 'accident' this past Monday, Ms. Hamilton and your suspicions about The Cadre."

"It's Anne," she corrected, looking at Mac. "To both of you."

"Okay, Anne," Griff agreed cheerfully. "Mac, did Hank tell you what the game plan was?"

"Yep," Mac said. "We're to go to The Oasis as soon as we're done with the police."

"Wait a minute!" Anne protested. "I need to go home at least long enough to get a change of clothing." She brushed her hands over her smoke-stained attire. "I can't keep wearing this! I'm filthy!"

"Hank has your house under surveillance." Griff's expression in the rear-view mirror turned serious. "One of our demolition experts is going over it. After your car was bombed, who's to say your house won't be next?"

"But my clothes-"

"We'll text Hank and ask him how he thinks we should handle that," Mac said. "Until we get an all-clear from him, we're not going anywhere near your house. We'll go to The Oasis and wait."

"But I have an interview with Katie Johnson's parents at four-thirty," Anne argued. She checked her watch. It was just past four. "I'd arranged to meet them at the downtown library. Rentals don't usually have GPS systems. Do you know how to get to the library? I can give you directions if you need them."

"She's keen on GPS," Mac growled and from the narrowed set of his eyes, Anne guessed this was another way to know when he was annoyed or even 'pissed off.' She'd have to remember the 'Scotty' thing.

And then, incredibly, a vision of what he might look like wearing a kilt and thick socks encasing those long, long legs flashed through her imagination, speeding up her heart. The image shifted so he was shirtless and holding up a shield and spear while a wild Highland wind blew through his thick hair, his defiant expression daring any challengers. Weariness threatened to overwhelm her, and she leaned her head against the window. *I'm losing it.*

"Anne?" Mac's voice seemed to come from far away. "Are you alright?"

"I'm fine," she lied. "What were we saying about GPS?"

But Griff only laughed and said, "I grew up in Knoxville and my parents are not only UT alums but retired professors. I know Knoxville, especially the downtown, better than most women know what's in their closets."

"That must be helpful," she said, and Mac's

abrupt laughter eased enough of her exhaustion to sit up and laugh with him as she tucked her imagination back into place.

"I, of course, have GPS on my phone, so no worries there, Anne," Griff said. "Who's Katie Johnson?"

Anne's brief happiness vanished, and she buried her nails into her palms. Where was her niece right now? What was she doing, thinking, feeling? *Please, Lord, let her be safe. Bring her home to us. Bring them all home to us.*

"Katie Johnson is a sixteen-year-old who vanished–would it be seven days now, Anne?" Mac said when Anne did not answer. "She got off her school bus but never made it home. She's Anne's niece. BP is involved through Tennessee Task Force to help find her and five other kids that have also gone missing in the past three weeks."

"Any chance Katie ran away?" Griffin asked, turning the car down High Street. "Kids that age often do."

"Never," Anne declared. "She would never hurt her family like that."

"Good enough for me," Griffin declared, pulling into a short-term parking spot by the library's front doors. "Text me when you're done, and I'll take you to The Oasis."

"The Oasis?" Anne repeated. "You mentioned that before, Mac. Is it some kind of club?"

"It's BP's local safe house," Mac explained, taking a packet of wipes from his jacket pocket. "Hold up. You missed some spots when you cleaned your face this morning after the blast."

He took one out and slowly moved the moist cloth around her face. She held herself very still, warming under his amber gaze and feather-soft touch, inhaling a scent of smoke and sandalwood, oddly comforting. For the first time in days, she felt some of the coiled tension in her shoulders melt away and realized she was no longer cold.

"That's better," he said, breaking the silence in the car. "Let's go meet the Johnsons. Maybe they've heard something."

They left the car to enter the library and found Katie's parents waiting in one of the smaller conference rooms. Introductions were made and the Johnsons asked how she was feeling, having read about her 'accident' in *Excelsior*. After assuring them she was fine, Anne explained how Stanley Harris knew of Brotherhood Protectors and what Mac's role would be in hopefully helping find Katie and the others. She thought they deserved to at least know that. They had heard nothing from Katie, nor had the other parents and Anne did not mention The Cadre.

"BP can't act as law enforcement," Mac explained to the tearful Johnsons. "But we can assist the police while doing our investigations.

And when it comes to helping find missing kids, BP will move heaven and earth to do just that."

His words brought on more tears, but they were more ones of relief than fear. The hour and a half spent with them was well-spent, he thought, and some of the fear stamped on their faces had faded.

Anne, on the other hand, looked as if she were holding herself together by sheer force of will. They made their goodbyes to the Johnsons and went outside where Mac's text brought Griff pulling up in the rental within minutes.

"Hank wants to meet with us tomorrow at nine," he said after they were settled in the back seat. "But he wants you to take it easy tonight. The fridge at The Oasis is full of prepared meals, so help yourself. I've got a job to do, so I'll see you tomorrow."

Mac nodded, his senses attuned to the woman beside him. Her ramrod-straight posture and stony expression worried him. She needed food and sleep as quickly as possible.

The Oasis was a large one-story house far enough out in the country for privacy but close enough to be downtown in minutes. Knoxville, Mac had learned, had many locations like that. The first block of this street held only three houses of varying size, but The Oasis set by itself in the cul-de-sac and Mac knew with its state-of-the-art security system it was a fortress within itself. For tonight, he thought, they should be safe.

Griff pulled into the driveway and up to the sidewalk leading to the front door. "Anne, do you by any chance have a packed suitcase at your home? I know a couple of reporters who always keep one at the ready in case they get a last-minute assignment and have to get on the road ASAP. As soon as I get word from Hank that your house is cleared, I can get it for you."

"I do," she said, taking her keys from her purse and handing them over. "It's in my bedroom in the closet."

"You'll have it tomorrow morning at the latest," Griff said as Mac opened the car door and helped her out. "Get some rest, both of you."

Inside, The Oasis' décor was homey with every amenity one could want. Anne's glance suggested her approval, but her expression remained weary. "What am I going to do about clothing until tomorrow?" she asked. "I can't sleep in these."

"BP has any number of women agents who sometimes stay here," Mac answered. "I think there are bathrobes and stuff you can use until Griff brings your suitcase. They use the second room on the left down that hall. I'll go warm up dinner."

She nodded and he watched her slowly make her way towards the bedrooms. A few minutes later he heard the faint rush of falling water. Hopefully, a shower, perhaps a glass of wine, and dinner would help Anne Hamilton relax. If she were wound any tighter, she would fall apart, and he didn't need or want to pick up the pieces. He headed to the kitchen, opened an IPA, and got to work.

By the time she'd joined him, he'd set the table, warmed up a mushroom casserole, and made the salad. "Something smells good," she said.

"Did you find everything you needed?" Mac turned from taking the rolls from the warming drawer and for a second, had to tighten his grip on the pan. Her hair gleamed with a freshly washed and dried sheen, and her features had relaxed a bit as if the water had washed away some of her weariness.

But the robe she wore. Saints preserve us, he needed a belt of whiskey. Maybe two.

The cobalt robe with lace on the collar and cuffs fell just above her knees, showing an incredible set of legs and he could only imagine what the rest of her looked like beneath the robe's soft fabric. Anne Hamilton's photo had not done her justice. She was a "right-fair looker" as his MacFarlane grandfather would say.

"Yes, thank you. There was quite a collection of big sleep shirts to choose from." Her gaze took in the red and white country-style kitchen and then the set table. "This looks nice."

"Would you care for a glass of wine?" he asked. "I just opened a bottle of Merlot."

"That would be fine," she said, sitting at the table.

He filled their glasses and served dinner. They ate in silence, and he was glad to see that except for the wine, she had seconds on everything. She did not argue with his offer to do KP. When he was finished, he brewed a pot of tea, filled a cup, and carried it into the living room where she sat on one of the sofas. She took the offered cup and smiled at him.

"You were good with Katie's parents," she said, sipping the Darjeeling. "They needed to hear something positive. Thank you."

"Brotherhood Protectors aims to please," he said, sitting beside her. "Good idea not to mention The Cadre to them. We're not sure they have Katie, and her parents are scared enough as it is."

She nodded, still smiling. "That's what Henry said."

"Henry was right," Mac said and added, "You should do that more often."

Her eyes narrowed and her smile vanished. "What? Say thank you?"

"Maybe." Mac eased into his father's brogue. "I was gonna say smile at me. You've not done that much since we met this morning. But having one's car blown up while being worried to death about her missing niece can make a lass a wee bit grouchy, don't you know."

Her fierce expression crumpled, and he caught her cup as it fell from her hand. He had just enough time to put it on the table and take her in his arms as she began to cry.

"Oh, my God," she choked, leaning into him, her tears soaking into his sweater. "Katie. What are we going to do if we don't find her? What am *I* going to do? I don't think I could bear it if she weren't in my life. If someone hurts her–"

"Shhh," he whispered, stroking her hair. It lay over her shoulders like a bolt of onyx silk and she smelled of roses and honeysuckle, calling up memories of summer nights in Inverness. "We're going to find her. I give you my word."

She raised her head to stare at him through tear-bright eyes. "Word of a Marine or BP?"

"Both," he said solemnly. "Throw in the word of a MacFarlane while we're at it. No way a three-way promise like that can fail."

"That's good to know." She settled against him and fell asleep.

He gathered her into his arms and carried her into the second bedroom, grateful to see she'd turned back the covers. As carefully as he could, he laid her on the bed and pulled the covers over her. After a moment, he slipped off her watch and put it on the nightstand, appreciating the softness of her wrist's skin beneath his fingers. He allowed himself a minute to study her face in sleep. Then he dimmed the lights, slipped from the room, and closed the door, leaving her to her much-needed rest.

CHAPTER 5

Thursday morning

The smell of freshly baked biscuits and brewing coffee wafted through the air, teasing Anne out of sleep. Light shimmered outside the window blinds' narrow slats, promising a warm, sunny October day. Propping herself on her elbows, she looked at her surroundings and panic seized her. Where was her furniture? Her cheval mirror? Her painting of Paris at twilight?

And why was she sleeping in a bathrobe she didn't own?

Then as yesterday's event rolled back into her memory, she sat up. Her meeting with Pastor Cole and Katie's parents. Spending most of the afternoon at police headquarters after her car exploded.

And all that time spent in the company of a very tall, off-the-charts good-looking former Marine named Mac. Heat seared Anne's cheeks as she recalled her down-right unfriendly and positively snarky attitude toward the man who'd been assigned to protect her and who had saved her life. Rude didn't even come close to describing her behavior towards him. She needed to apologize.

Another glance around the room brought a sigh of relief as she spotted her travel suitcase by a rocking chair. The bedside digital clock on the nightstand showed it was 7:25 am. From under it, she took the folded sheet of paper, flipped it open, and read the following printed message.

Hope you slept well and like a hash brown casserole. Mac.

Suddenly aware of just how hungry she was, she rolled out of bed, took trousers and a cable-knit sweater along with her underwear and make-up bag from her suitcase, and headed to the shower. Just having her clothes made her feel almost normal. She made good use of the soaps and shampoos lining the shower box wall and noted again several women's bathrobes hanging on wall hooks. By the time she'd dried and braided her hair, and applied a light-make-up, Anne was so hungry, she was sure she could have found the kitchen blindfolded. She made her bed and hung up the robe, just like her mother had taught her, and let the smell of breakfast propel her to the kitchen.

"Good morning," she greeted as Mac pulled a pan of biscuits from the oven. "Thank you for the note."

He returned her smile. "Good morning," he said. "Sleep well?"

"Like a rock," Anne told him, helping herself to the coffee. "Does BP always keep a supply of women's bathrobes as well as sleepshirts here?"

"Yep." He opened the oven again and pulled out a long baking dish. "This casserole has sausage and cheese as well as potatoes," he announced. "I noticed you had part of a sausage biscuit yesterday, so I guess you're not a vegetarian."

"I'm not, but Katie is." The memory halted Anne's words for a moment and she took a quick sip of her coffee, wondering how her favorite girl was holding up. Probably giving her abductors a very hard time. *You go, Katie.*

He filled two plates and set them on the table. "Let's eat before we start talking business," he suggested. "Our meeting with Hank is at nine o'clock and I don't think well on an empty stomach."

"Me either." She took her place at the table and when he was seated, she said, "I'm sorry I was such a bitch yesterday."

Golden lights flickered in his eyes. "You mean you were a bitch because your CI was killed when someone tried to run you over and later blew up your car all in a matter of two days? Let's not forget someone abducted your niece, you got banged and bruised when you hit the pavement, not once but twice, had almost no sleep, not to mention ruined your manicure?"

His on-point description made her smile. "Something like that," she agreed, after savoring a bite of the casserole.

"Sounds like good reasons to be a bitch to me," he said. "But your apology is accepted."

They ate in comfortable silence for a few minutes before Anne spoke. "How long do you think it will take for my house to be cleared of possible bombs or listening devices? Could we be staying here at The Oasis for quite a while?"

He cocked his head, as if considering how to answer her question. "Hard to say," he finally said. "It's like we said yesterday. If The Cadre found a way to plant the bomb in your car without you knowing it, they probably know where you live. And even if your house has been pronounced clean today, they could go there at any time, if they've been there at all. You haven't mentioned any pets."

"I don't have any," Anne said regretfully. "I keep such crazy hours I've always thought it wouldn't be fair to have a dog or cat waiting for me." Another thought occurred to her. "Is BP going to be watching my house until this is over?"

"Yes ma'am," Mac said, putting more of the casserole on her plate. "Twenty-four-seven. Do you think you have enough clothing for the duration? That bag didn't look like it could hold more than a few days' worth and most women I know tend to overpack. You know, 'I'll take this just in case' and it feels as if they've packed enough for a month. Yours didn't feel like that."

His description surprised her. "You seem to know a lot about women and their packing habits."

His wide grin spiked her pulse. "I have sisters," he said. "Believe me, it was a matter of survival on learning how women think and dress. Came in handy when I started dating. Do you have siblings?"

His question stripped the warmth from her skin, leaving a sensation of loss. "Two sisters and two brothers, all younger than me," she said. "But we don't talk much."

Her tone must have suggested changing the subject would be a good idea because he nodded and asked, "Would you like another biscuit? It's going to be a busy day and we need to keep up our strength." He switched to his now familiar brogue to add, "At least that's what my Scottish grandmothers always say."

His comical expression chased some of the sorrow from her heart. "Are Scottish grandmothers like Italian ones are supposed to be?" she asked, taking another biscuit and slathering it in butter. "Always telling everyone Eat! Eat! You too skinny!"

"You have no idea," he said, and she joined in his laughter as they finished their meal.

"Will it be safe to go to *Excelsior* and get my laptop?" she asked as they cleared the table and loaded the dishwasher. "I have files and notes of some of the work I did with Henry. We might find something useful."

He liked her use of the word "we", hoping this was a sign she'd accepted the inevitability of BP's involvement in her case and her life. Savvy reporter she might be, she needed to be very cautious in her desire to find The Cadre and rescue her niece and the others.

And be more than just a little afraid. "We should be safe," he said. "But you should call and let them know we're coming."

She nodded and left, leaving him to wonder at her silence about her siblings. His sixth sense—which his grandmothers swore he had—told him there was something painfully sad in Anne Hamilton's past between her and her family. Best not to ask. When she was ready to tell him, she would. At least he hoped so.

"Hello, the house!" Griff Tyler's ringing voice

called out. "I'm getting the meeting set up. You guys ready?"

"On the way," Mac answered as he headed for the office. Anne was already there, seated on one of the long sofas the BP crew preferred, studying her phone. She looked up as Mac entered and said, "I've had a text from Pastor Cole. He says there's someone he wants us to meet. They'll be at *Sophia's* coffee shop on The Square at 1:30. I told him we would be there."

"Works for me," Mac agreed. "Maybe it's that person he mentioned yesterday. That was quick work on his part."

The computer's oversize screen flashed, and Hank Patterson's image filled the widescreen.

"Good morning, Anne," Hank greeted. "I trust you spent a comfortable night?"

"Yes, thank you," she said. "I'm feeling much better and I'm ready to get started on today's business, whatever that is. I'd like to work on learning more about where my niece Katie and the other kids might be."

"Sergeant Grant Miller from KPD faxed a list of all the teens who've gone missing and are presumed runaways over the last year," Griff announced. "He also faxed over the particulars of the six who are most recently gone. It has their parents' contact information, their schools, and known hangouts."

"Grant Miller helped BP out on a case involving an endangered child earlier this spring and earned a much-deserved promotion because of it," Mac explained to Anne. "He's our point person at KPD."

"Let's review what we know," Hank suggested, "and what Henry Cooper told you, Anne."

"According to Henry, the presence of The Cadre was only just confirmed," Anne said. "There's been suspicion, but the street sources stopped talking to the police because they're so afraid of The Cadre. Katie Johnson's parents told us yesterday that so far, neither they nor the other kids' parents have heard a word from anyone. No threats or ransom demands. It's like their children just vanished."

"I spent this morning reviewing some of what we know about The Cadre," Griff said. "And I know the local police force is damned good at what they do. Do we know why it took them so long to confirm The Cadre's presence?"

"Because when The Cadre moves into a new area, they do it quietly, without fanfare or making trouble, scouting the lay of the land, as it were," Mac explained. "They make 'friends' with some of the local powerhouses, convincing them they'll be stronger by working with The Cadre. For those that won't, they start with acts of intimidation and threats until they've taken over completely. And when it comes to trafficking kids, they usually find recent runaways or kids who've been on the streets for a while. They court them, so to speak, and trick them with offers of great jobs in modeling or entertainment with a chance to travel, be independent, and make piles of money."

"But the six missing kids weren't on the street or runaways," Anne objected, taking the sheet from Griff. "They wouldn't be likely to respond to such offers. Why would The Cadre change the kind of kids they select?"

"The demographics on what type of victim the pedophiles and abusers want is changing all the time," Hank said. "And there are hundreds of thousands of them out there, worldwide. All races, ethnicities, and economic brackets have one thing in common. They're pedophiles."

"But I know these kids," Anne said, looking up from the sheet. "At least I know who they are. Every fall, *Excelsior* holds a city-county-wide writing contest for high-school juniors. Six winners are selected from among the hundreds of entries we receive. The prize is a summer internship at *Excelsior*. Normally, I'm on the judging committee, but because I know Katie, I was disqualified this year. *Excelsior* announced the winners a month before Marie Wallis, the first kid who went missing three weeks ago. She and these other kids were the winners. I met them and their parents at a celebration the paper held, and I think they all liked me. Do you think it would be ok for me to talk to their parents?"

"If they and their kids like you, I'll bet they'll be more than grateful for your help," Hank said. "But we'll check with Grant Miller just to be sure."

"Is this writing contest a big deal?" Griff asked. "You said you got hundreds of entries?"

"We did," Anne said. "*Excelsior* has been holding this contest for at least fifty years. We set very high standards for writing, and to be chosen as one of the six winners is a great honor. Several well-known journalists got their start there."

"And you were one of them," Mac guessed.

"I was," Anne admitted, her face warming. "It's what led me to work there and begin my career in investigative journalism."

"A career built on honesty, integrity, and hard work," Hank praised. "Or so Stanley Harris told me. But remember this, Anne. We're operating on the belief that The Cadre targeted you as well as your friend Henry. He knew that they were trafficking teens in this area and told you. And I have no doubt they know it was you who wrote that story about them trafficking kids in Gainesville last spring."

Mac watched the color drain from her face as Hank's words sank in. "Henry said the same thing," she said after a moment. "That I'd been 'made' which is why my editor called you after the accident, asking for your help."

"And we're glad to supply it," Hank said. "So, Mac is going to be pretty much glued to your side until The Cadre is found and stopped."

"Agreed," Mac said firmly. "When they're establishing power in a new area, The Cadre will do just about anything to get and keep it, and they don't care who they hurt. One of the first things we need to figure out is other is why The Cadre targeted these six kids in particular. We don't have any proof yet they have them, but I'll bet you dollars to donuts that they do."

"But all I know is what Henry told me," Anne insisted. "That they'd brought in guns and drugs and possibly had those six kids. He never named names of people he thought were in The Cadre. I don't think he knew any, at least not yet."

"But they don't know that he didn't," Mac countered. "Them believing you know something was reason enough to blow up your car."

"Anne, could Henry have talked to anyone else besides you?" Hank asked. "Someone else he trusted?"

Her fearful expression faded, and Mac could almost see the wheels turning in her head. "Not that I recall," she said slowly. "He said he had one "snitch" left who would talk to him, but never gave me a name. I'll check my notes on my laptop after we pick it up at *Excelsior.*"

"Then that's where to start," Hank agreed. "Anne, is there going to be a problem with Mac being with you at all times?"

"No," she replied. "I've had enough sleep that my brain realizes how dangerous all of this is. Running on adrenaline can mess with your thinking."

"Sticking to her like glue," Mac promised. "Or a Scottish cocklebur."

"Be safe," Hank ordered, but he was smiling, and his image faded from the screen.

"Okay," Mac said. "The first order of business before we meet with Pastor Cole will be to go to *Excelsior* to pick up Anne's laptop. My main concern is getting her in and out of the building without being seen."

"And we need to check on your truck," Anne added with mock solemnity. "Poor Mac. You looked so forlorn when Officer Tucker said they had to keep it for a while."

"No one gets between a MacFarlane and his truck," Griff announced. "No one. But no worries about getting Anne into the building. I've got that taken care of."

"Really?" Mac said. "I'm almost afraid to ask how."

"Then don't." Griff winked at Anne. "It will be a surprise."

"I was afraid you'd say that," Mac sighed. "I hate surprises."

CHAPTER 6

"Where the hell did you get a garbage truck?" Mac shouted over the engine's clattering roar as they bumped along. "Someone needs to check out the shocks."

Anne could not hold back her laughter. "That picture I snapped of you when you saw this thing parked in the driveway at The Oasis will make us all rich," she said. "Griff, how did you persuade the sanitation department to let you borrow this monster?" The truck was enormous but the front seat while just big enough for two, made a tight squeeze for three and she was sandwiched between the two men.

And seated this close to Mac, she could enjoy the smell of soap mingled with a faint, woodsy scent, emanating from him. It was soothing, yet exciting and suited him perfectly.

"Being from Knoxville, I know people in just about every walk of life," Griff boasted. "Let's say I called in a favor. The Cadre isn't going to suspect you'll be traveling in a garbage truck. I'll park this bad boy next to the dumpsters behind *Excelsior* so you can slip in the back doors."

Anne looked him over. "I've never seen a sanitation worker with green hair wearing pillow-stuffed overalls, but I don't think The Cadre will 'make' you as being a member of BP in that outfit."

"Hope not," Griff said. "My mother taught in UT's drama department for years. She let me help out backstage during shows which is where I got good with makeup."

"Really?" Anne said. "What did your father teach?"

"Nutrition. His lasagna will knock you on your butt."

"He's a man of many talents, our Griff," Mac stated. "And a computer genius to boot."

"That I am," Griff" agreed, pulling into *Excelsior*'s back lot. "Text me when you're ready."

Inside *Excelsior*, Anne introduced Mac to her colleagues as a visiting friend and watched him work his charm on them, especially the women, and wondered if he was at ease in every situation. He might have known these people all his life.

"Girlfriend, if that man is single, you better jump on him before I do," Celeste Taylor said, coming from the break room to give Anne her laptop case. They had a standing agreement they would watch each other's computers if they had been left at the office. "Is he your new squeeze?"

"Just a friend," Anne said, taking the case. Celeste was a born matchmaker.

"Hope it's a friend with privileges," Celeste murmured as Mac moved toward them. "With legs like that, you're going to need a long bed."

"Hush," Anne warned as Mac joined them. She made a mental note to pick up smelling salts to keep in her desk. Celeste's star-struck expression suggested she might need them if she and Mac met again.

"Anne, I need to see you and your friend, please," Stanley Harris called from the doorway of his spacious office off the newsroom. He and Anne had agreed not to tell the others of his call to Brotherhood Protectors or who Mac was.

"Sure," Anne answered, maneuvering between her colleagues' oversize desks. Mac moved behind her with a silent tread that was unsettling. Once inside his office, Stanley closed the door and Anne said, "Stanley Harris, meet–"

"We've met," Mac interrupted. "I wasn't available when you and Mr. Harris called BP on Monday and spoke to Hank. I called him when I knew I was assigned to the case, and we had our own face-to-face meeting. Good to see you, again Mr. Harris."

"You didn't tell me you'd called him," Anne accused.

"You didn't ask." The twinkle in Mac's eyes was undeniably mischievous, and she murmured, "touché" as Stanley waved them into the chairs facing his desk. When they were seated, he said, "We have a development. Anne, I know you worked with Henry for years, but what did you know about him? Did he ever tell you how he came to be on the streets or his life before that?"

"No," Anne sighed. "I asked him several times over the years, but he refused to talk about it, so I stopped asking. I'm not even sure if he had any family. Why?"

"Someone left this at the front desk this morning." Stanley took an unsealed envelope from inside his jacket and gave it to her. Her name was scrawled across the front and after peering inside, she took out two long, silver chains with rectangle medallions dangling from them. Recognition shivered over her as she held them up. "Oh, my," she whispered. "Dog tags."

Beside her, Mac took and held them up to stare at the printing stamped on the chains. "I'll be damned," he said softly. "Henry was a Marine twenty years ago."

"I was hoping *Excelsior* could pay to have Henry

buried," Stanley said slowly. "We owe it to him, if only for saving Anne's life. But since he's a veteran that changes things considerably. Lt. MacFarlane, can you contact the DOD or the VA about finding his family? There's a veterans' cemetery here in Knoxville they could use if they want."

"Absolutely," Mac said in a tone Anne had never heard him use. Was this the famous loyalty that veterans shared with all other veterans, even if they'd never met? To always stand by each other, even in death? One look at his face confirmed her belief. "Where did you say this was found?" she asked.

"Someone left it on one of the receptionists' desks in the front lobby," Stanley said. "But since everyone uses coded cards to get in, whoever left it either has one or just followed someone inside. I've had the supervisors of every department talk to their people and no one left it, so it was someone else."

"Someone from The Cadre, you mean," Anne said softly.

"We don't know that," Mac pointed out. "Maybe it's a street friend of Henry's who knows he was a Marine and wanted to be sure you knew it too. But it's even more reason to always be on guard."

"Exactly," Stanley said. "Be warned, MacFarlane. She's on leave, but she's as stubborn as a mule. She's going to keep on investigating this no matter how I warn her or tell her what to do, so try to keep her from getting into too much trouble."

"I'll keep an eye on her," Mac said, returning the dog tags to Anne, who put them in her purse. "You hired me to protect her and that's what I'm going to do. Count on it."

"Well, I'm glad the two of you have got that settled," Anne announced as they stood. "I feel like a package of goods being haggled over."

"Best package I've got," Stanley pronounced, coming around his desk to kiss her on the cheek. "I don't want to lose her."

The men shook hands, before Anne could reach for her laptop, Mac picked it up and slung the strap over his shoulder. "I've got this," he said. "Your hands are still banged up."

"I can manage to carry my laptop," Anne insisted. "I've got scrapes, not broken bones."

"Sure, and it's the Scottish gentleman in me," he quipped. "A lass shouldn't be saying no to that."

"Oh, fine," Anne said. "Let's go talk to Pastor Cole."

They had reached the elevators when Mac took out his phone and scanned the screen. "Griff says he'll meet us behind the building shortly, but it won't be in the garbage truck."

"Wait a minute." Anne grabbed his arm. "You're not going to try to stop me from finding Katie and the others or find out who killed Henry, are you?"

Her protector peered down at her. "Do I look crazy to you? I said I'd keep an eye on you. I didn't say anything about stopping you from doing whatever you're already planning on doing. Because come hell or high water, you're gonna do whatever it takes to find Katie Johnson and the others and find out who killed Henry Cooper."

He took her hands, and she felt his strength flowing through her, warm and alive, making her aware, not for the first time, of just how dangerously attractive he was. That smile could lead a girl to walk willingly into a garden of temptation and never look back.

"And I'm going to be with you," he said softly, determination glittering in his eyes. "Every step of the way."

CHAPTER 7

"Did you have any idea that Henry Cooper was a veteran?" Mac asked.

They were on their way to meet with Pastor Cole and his friend in Mac's truck. They'd gone back to The Oasis for lunch after Griff had picked them up from *Excelsior* in a floral delivery van that he'd "borrowed" with the request "not to ask." From there, they'd gone to the police station where Mac's truck waited, newly washed. Anne couldn't remember the last time she saw a man look so happy.

"No," she said thoughtfully. "He never mentioned anything about his past or personal life.

At times I thought maybe he didn't trust me and kept it to himself."

"He trusted you enough with the information he gave you," Mac said. "But sometimes veterans don't like talking about themselves or what they experienced. Too much stuff that happened that only other veterans would understand."

Something in his voice quickened Anne's reporter's curiosity but she took the time to ask with the greatest respect, "Even if there are people who love the veteran and want to try to understand and to help them?"

"Yeah," he answered. "Even then."

Now they were headed back to Knoxville and *Sophia's* coffee shop. It was a popular place, appealing to all ages with a seasonal menu and live music on the weekend. Mac found a parking place in the State Street Garage, making it an easy walk back. Out on the sidewalk, he offered her his arm and said, "My lady?"

"You're too kind, sir." Beneath his coat, she felt a muscled strength and confidence. A sense of safety swept over her, and she wondered at his description of veterans. What had he seen during his years in service? What had he seen or experienced? Given the short time they'd known each other, she doubted he would tell her.

But it felt like something she should know.

And when this was all over, she was going to find out.

Sophia's was still crowded when they entered, but Mac's height gave him the advantage to search the room. "There they are," he said. "At that booth in the back."

"Oh my," she murmured as they moved between the tables. "Where in the world did Pastor Cole find *that*?"

"Ms. Hamilton, Lt. MacFarlane, this is Barclee," Pastor Cole introduced as they slid into the booth facing him and his companion. "Barclee, these are the people I told you about and the ones I hope you'll help."

Pastor Cole was immaculate in his clerical garb and black overcoat, but Barclee's outfit was nothing short of bizarre. An oversized orange puff jacket covered in sequins made it hard to determine Barclee's weight. A pink, tight-fitting knitted cap covered whatever hair Barclee had, and it was impossible to tell his race beneath his mud-smeared face. His filthy, high-necked maroon sweater and battered jeans needed a good washing, and recalling Henry's recent disheveled appearance, excitement shimmied over Anne's skin. Was this Henry's 'snitch'? The one who'd confirmed his suspicions about The Cadre's presence? He'd never mentioned the names of his street contacts. "Keeps them and you safe by not telling," he often told her.

But at least she knew Henry was male. Over-sized sunglasses covered the upper portion of Barclee's face, making it impossible to guess what gender they claimed. So did the boxing gloves. Either a man's or a woman's hands could be hidden there, and she wondered how they and Pastor Cole had met.

"The God-Man says you need Barclee's help," Barclee rasped. "Sometimes Barclee helps, some-times not." Nothing in the voice provided a clue as to gender or age.

"We are looking for a lost girl," Mac began. "Katie Johnson. We think The Cadre had her about seven days ago." He believed in cutting to the chase. "Did Pastor Cole tell you that?"

"The God-Man did," Barclee agreed. "Many youths on the streets Cadre might want. Cadre people very, very dangerous."

"What can you tell us about Katie Johnson?" Anne struggled to control her impatience. "She's only sixteen, and there are five other teens who are missing as well. What can you tell us about The Cadre possibly snatching them? We know they didn't run away."

"Many people in other places want pretty kids." Barclee's expression remained unreadable, his tone almost sing-song. "Much talk of pretty kids being moved to Hot 'Lanta very soon. Some others not so pretty are still wanted for work in underground factories, farms, and cheap labor. Street says Cadre hides these six pretty kids not so far away until time to go. Places policemen do not know about. Pretty ones to become playthings, not work hard labor on farms. Cadre makes much money to buy more guns and drugs from selling these pretty kids."

Recalling one of the first stories she'd done when she started working at *Excelsior,* Anne's excitement increased. "You mean playthings for sex," she said. The word playthings left a foul taste in her mouth, and she could barely get out her next question. "Being used for prostitution?"

"The pretty writer lady is wise," Barclee said.

"When," Mac retorted. "When will they be moved?" His voice took on an edge that should have made Barclee nervous, but Barclee only smiled at them.

"Soon," Barclee said.

"How do you know that?" Anne demanded. "Other than Pastor Cole bringing you here, why should we believe you?

"Street people tell Barclee many things," Barclee purred. "No one notices homeless people. Like being invisible. No one notices except to chase homeless people away. And because we are invisible, we see, and hear strange things, no one else sees or hears. People, they tell Barclee these things. Barclee tells the God-Man."

"Barclee, with what you've heard, when might these kids be moved?" Cole asked. "We really need to know."

"Early next week," Barclee told them after a long pause. "Maybe sooner. Barclee will find out when and tell the God-Man. Barclee promises to help the tall man and the pretty writer lady. Tell them everything Barclee learns and Barclee always keeps their word. But the tall man and pretty writer lady must be careful. Cadre knows of your quest."

"Who told them?" Mac demanded.

"And why would you help us?" Anne added, still unwilling to trust this strange creature. "What is it worth to you?"

Barclee's chuckle slid into a long, slow laugh, eerie in its depth. Beside her, Mac stiffened as if in preparation to defend them.

"Henry Cooper," Barclee said at last. "Henry Cooper told Barclee that would tell pretty writer lady about Cadre and missing kids. Barclee and Henry are friends, help each other, and help others like them. Cadre found out Henry knew about them, so they killed him. Tried to kill you too, pretty writer lady. Barclee will help you find them. Save the children for Henry's sake."

"If Barclee gives you their word, then you can believe them," Pastor Cole said. Anne noticed the man's easy use of gender-neutral pronouns. "Barclee has always been honest with me and has brought me news about street activity for several years, especially when it might impact my congregation."

Anne's phone trilled, and she eased it out of her coat pocket to glance at the screen. Her heart plummeted, and she looked at the men around the table. "I need to take this," she said, sliding out of the booth. "It's personal."

"I'll come with you," Mac said starting to get up, but Anne gently pushed him back.

"It's personal," she repeated. "I saw a police officer right outside. I'll stay near him, I promise. Thank you, Pastor Cole. Thank you, Barclee. I'll be right back."

She hurried outside, the phone still buzzing. Watching the officer, she hit accept and said, "Mom? Is everything alright?"

"More importantly, are you alright? A friend told me about the accident." Her mother's soft voice was a blessing but did nothing to slow Anne's mounting anxiety. Her mother only called when she was completely alone, or something was wrong, or both.

"I'm fine, Mom. How is da–how is everyone?" Anne followed the officer from the square as he turned a corner and headed down Gay Street, quickly covering several blocks. Mac, she thought, was going to kill her.

"We're all fine, dear," her mother assured. "I can't talk long."

"I understand," Anne said quickly. "Mom, have you heard anything about your neighbors hiring young people to work on the farms? Or seen any strangers about?"

"Talk to Amos," her mother whispered. "He'll be at The Market tomorrow for Third Friday. He always knows everything." There was a brief pause. "Your father is coming. I have to go."

"Text me," Anne pleaded, but the call ended, and she fought the desire to throw the phone. Instead, she shoved it into her coat pocket and turned to see a scowling Mac coming toward her from at least ten blocks up. Sighing, she headed in his direction. She better have a good explanation prepared because the man looked seriously pissed.

And Lord, help. Even pissed off, he was just too good-looking. If The Cadre ever caught sight of that expression, they'd be hot-footing it back to Chicago the first chance they got. The thought nearly made her smile.

So she didn't hear the approaching car or see the heavily bearded man in a half mask jump out of the back seat until he'd grabbed her upper arm.

"Come on, bitch," he hissed, struggling to drag

Anne back to the idling car. "My boss ain't happy with your snooping and making trouble for him."

Rage exploded in a red haze across Anne's field of vision. Rage for what happened to Henry, to Katie and the kids, rage at the man she once called 'Dad' and hadn't spoken to in years. And rage at what was happening to her right now.

"Let me go, you sick, perverted son-of-a bitch!" she screamed, taking a huge step back. It caught the man off-guard, and she jerked her arm free while reaching into her other pocket for the pepper spray she always carried. She pushed the nozzle, spraying him in the face. The mixture of ground chili peppers and onion juice stung her own eyes and nose and left her gasping for air while her screaming assailant stumbled backward. From the car's still-open back door, a long arm pulled him inside. The door slammed, and with tires screeching, the car took off, sideswiping an SUV in its haste to escape just as Mac pounded up to her and jerked her against his chest.

"What the hell did you think you were doing?" he shouted. "You weren't supposed to leave the square!"

Snatching her phone from her pocket, Anne held it up. "I was talking to my mother!"

CHAPTER 8

Thursday evening

"I came on board this mission to keep you safe, not to have you get yourself killed by wandering off!" Mac shouted. "What the hell were you thinking?" He'd left the overhead dome of his truck on because he wanted her to see just how very mad he was.

"I followed that police officer so if I needed help, I could yell, 'Help!'" Anne returned his shout. Anger darkened her green eyes to a brilliant sheen of jade and her lips–which he had the strangest desire to kiss–pulled together in a tight, red line. "And I got away, didn't I?"

"Only because you were damned lucky and had that pepper spray," Mac retorted, turning his truck onto the highway and heading south for Townsend. An earlier call to his BP friend Parker Evans gained permission to use his family's compound as an operating base and Griff had brought Anne's suitcase to the police station from The Oasis. After the attack, Mac didn't think it was safe to spend the night there. It was too close to the city and Sergeant Miller had agreed with that plan when they met with him to file a report on Anne's attack.

"No doubt now that someone is watching you all the time," Miller said when she'd finished giving her statement. "Given that your attacker said his boss is not happy with you, Ms. Hamilton, you need to find a place where they're not likely to find you. Damn ballsy of them to attack you on the street in the middle of the day."

"What am I supposed to do? Hide until all this is over?" Anne had demanded.

"You need to stay with Lt. MacFarlane at least when you're in public," Miller returned. "Let him do his job and we'll do ours."

Now, as they sped through the early evening light towards Townsend, Mac's gaze moved between the approaching traffic and the rearview mirror. Griff was two cars behind, still driving the floral delivery truck. Mac had not wanted him to hear the argument he knew he and Anne would have. From the look on their faces when they exited the police station, Griff had agreed.

But even now, in the relative safety of his truck, Mac could not relax his grip on the steering wheel or slow the thundering of his heart as images of the laughing Sayyid children flooded his brain. Ahmed, the eldest trying so hard to be the man of the family. Little Damsa, his dancer. Smiling Baddar. Shy Arezo. Bahil who loved American football.

He should have saved them. But how do you stop monsters on motorcycles, brandishing automatic rifles?

You should have taken them inside the cafe, the old voices whispered. *They'd still be alive if you had.*

Not your fault, argued his mantra. *Not your fault.* But his anger was building.

I should have followed Anne. It was my fault I didn't. She could have been abducted or worse.

"What was so damn important you had to go outside to take that phone call from your mother?" he asked aloud, switching off the dome light. "Couldn't you have taken it in the ladies' room or something?"

"Okay, I'm sorry, alright?" The irritation in her voice was all too plain. "Why are you still so angry?"

"Because if I'd stayed with the Sayyid children, they'd be alive instead of being gunned down outside the café!" Mac roared, unable to stop the cascading anger and guilt pouring out of him. "I don't need your death on my conscience too! If I'd stayed with you, those f'ing bastards wouldn't have tried to grab you, so you keep your sweet ass right beside mine! Have you got that?"

In the following silence, his labored breathing thundered in his ears, and he could feel the sweat soaking through his shirt and jacket. He fixed a hard, unblinking gaze at the horizon, praying his fragile control wouldn't shatter and he would start weeping in front of this woman he'd just met.

"Who are the Sayyid children?" Anne's voice seemed to come from far away instead of beside him. "Are they someone you knew in Afghanistan? Did something happen to them?"

"Look, I'm sorry I lost my temper." Mac bit off the words. "My bad. And I don't want to talk about Afghanistan, okay? We're almost there."

He pulled into the compound's open gates, and they closed behind them. He'd barely shut off the truck when he was out, crossing the short space from the driveway to the front porch and unlocking the door. Somehow, he found his way to the gym, ripping off his coat and shirts as he went, dropping them who the hell knows where or cares?

And then it was just a bare-chested him and the punching bag and he was slamming his ungloved fists into it with all the force of his rage and sorrow, only dimly aware he was chanting the children's names over and over. Ahmed. Damsa. Arezo.

Baddar. Bahil. Lily. The sweat poured over his body in wave after wave of anger that had erupted without warning. Ahmed. Damsa. Arezo. Baddar. Bahil. Lily.

His fists continued to punish the bag until he collapsed against it, wrapping his arms around it as it swayed against him and he dug his feet into the floor to hold himself up. His burning lungs labored to pull in the air until at last his breathing and heart slowed and his arms relaxed. Stepping back from the bag, he turned to find Anne straddling a weight bench, her eyes wide not only with concern but compassion as well.

"Who were they?" she asked.

"Who was who?" He walked to the towel stand and grabbed one from the stack to wipe down his face and chest.

"The names you were chanting," she said, swinging her legs around. She went to the small refrigerator and removed a bottle of water, stopping to grab another towel and bring it to him. "Were those children you knew in Afghanistan? You said their name was Sayyid."

"Yeah." He twisted off the cap and threw it aside to chug down half the bottle's contents. "They were kids I knew there."

"And they were killed." It was a statement, not a question. "Look, I'm not trying to play therapist or anything, but do you want to tell me about them?"

Her hand inside of his was soft, as she led him to the weight bench where they sat. After a moment, Mac said, "There were a few of us Marines left in this one village. We were working on trying to get some of the men who'd acted as translators to America with their families. Mohammed Sayyid, their father, had been killed, but he had a brother here who was working with the State Department to get them out of there. Some of us in my unit would take turns walking the Sayyid children to and from school because it wasn't always safe."

He paused to take another sip of water and said, "This one morning, the kids were particularly hungry. They never had quite enough to eat so we stopped at this little café. It was packed and even though I told them to come inside, they wanted to stay outside and watch this old man doing magic tricks. Ahmed–he was ten years old, the oldest, and considered himself to be the man of the family– told me it was his job to watch his siblings and mine was to go get the food, so to be quick about it."

"Sounds like Ahmed was bossy," Anne suggested.

"That he was," Mac managed a chuckle. "But while I was inside, motorcyclists with Kalashnikovs came by, and opened fire, spraying the square. All the kids were killed, along with at least twenty other people. The shock of losing all her children was so bad that Irina, their mother had a heart attack and died."

"Ahmed. Arezo. Damsa. Baddar. Bahil," Anne recited. Reverence colored her tone, and she might have been praying. "Good names for good children," she said softly. "But Lily doesn't sound like an Afghani name."

"Lily was the youngest sister of my friend and fellow BP comrade Parker Evans," Mac explained. "She was snatched when she was four years old while we were at a country fair. We never found her or had a word of her. And I'd rather not talk about that right now if you don't mind."

Understanding dawned in her eyes. "That's why you joined the Tennessee Task Force. To help protect and rescue children."

"Yep," he agreed. At this point, he wasn't sure how much more talking he could or wanted to do.

"Your hands are skinned and bleeding," she whispered, pressing the towel over his fingers. "I've got a salve that will help them."

"I love a woman who is always prepared," he said.

She nodded and her gaze shifted to his left shoulder. "You were wounded," she said, gently touching the scarred skin. "Did this happen while you were trying to save the Sayyids?"

"Some of them," he said again. "I was last in line at the café and first out the door when those bastards rode up and started firing. The bullets hit me when I dived to save the kids. Or thought I was saving them."

"And that's why you were so angry at me," she said. "You weren't there when that guy grabbed me. You weren't there when I needed you. I was by myself, and you weren't there to stop the attack."

"Give the little lady a cigar," Mac intoned, moving his hands away from hers.

"I am so sorry," she whispered, reaching up to push back a strand of his sweat-soaked hair. "Sorry, I left you when I should have stayed outside *Sophia's* and sorry for everything else."

Her rose and honeysuckle scent filled his head, sweet and intoxicating, like an invitation to the best celebration ever from the prettiest woman he'd ever met. He'd wondered too long what her mouth would taste like, and damning himself for being a romantic, sentimental Scottish fool, he took her in his arms and kissed her.

Her response was all he could have wanted. Urgent, needful, demanding. Against his chest, her heartbeat was a wild staccato rhythm, and her rapid breathing was a love song in his ears. Groaning, he deepened his kiss, tasting something faintly sweet on her lips, and he thought the desire pulsing in his veins would devour him. "Anne," he whispered. "Anne."

But then she pulled back, scooting away from

him and lowering her gaze. "Wow," she said softly. "I didn't see that coming."

You ass, Mac. Now you've gone and scared her. "I'm sorry," he muttered. "That was way out of line."

"I was talking about me," she said and looked him in the face. Pink stained her cheeks in a way no rouge ever could, and her mouth had a freshly kissed look, but she favored him with a tiny smile. "And I'm not sorry. I wanted that as much as I think you did. So, before this gets out of hand, let's go upstairs and after I get you that salve for your hands, let's see what we can put together for dinner, and I'll tell you why it was so important for me to talk to my mother."

CHAPTER 9

Earlier that afternoon

"We don't like failure, Franklin." The man behind the desk declared, his voice bouncing off the windowless concrete walls. Except for the small penlight he held, the room was completely dark. "This was a simple enough assignment–grab the Hamilton woman and bring her to me."

"Shit, the bitch pepper sprayed me!" A sweating, shirtless Tyrel Franklin protested as a man in a mask like the one he'd worn earlier, pulled his wrists behind his back and bound them with rope, while the other man stood to the side, knife in hand, waiting. "I had a hold of her arm good and tight–"

"Yet she got away," the voice interrupted. "If you

can't do something that simple, you are not to be trusted. Where is Anne Hamilton now?"

"Don't know," Franklin grumbled. His eyes still burned from the pepper spray, and he couldn't smell a thing. "It's not like she gave me her address."

The man with the knife slapped him, hard. Franklin yelped and struggled to break free, but his bonds were too tight, cutting into his wrists' flesh and he had to force himself not to cry out again. "I'm sorry," he whimpered. "I'm sorry."

"You will find her within the next twenty-four hours and let me know where she is. If you fail, you die. You have been warned." The man nodded at the one holding the knife. "Do the L," he commanded.

"No wait! I'll find her!" Franklin cried as he heard the soft 'snick' of a switchblade snapping open. The smell of his sweat was making him gag. "Maybe she'll go back to the newspaper and–"

His screams bounced off the walls as the knife slowly carved the letter L into the flesh of his upper right arm. Something caustic had been rubbed onto the knife's blade and it burned like the flames of hell his preacher grandpappy had warned he would face if he didn't change his ways. The grip on his arms relaxed and his knees buckled, taking him to the floor, sobbing.

"Get him out of here," the man behind the desk ordered. The others did not wait to hear his command issued again. They knew better. Hauling the still sobbing Franklin to his feet, they dragged him from the room and shut the door.

Alone, the man released a volley of curses. He'd been a fool to even try to trust Franklin and couldn't afford to wait twenty-four hours. He'd kill Franklin himself and get someone else to find Anne Hamilton. As much as he would like to kill her himself, someone else had demanded that pleasure.

She'd made BAB look like fools seven years ago with her article, dissolving their plans for a better, stronger Tennessee like sugar in hot tea before they took their mission to the next level. Anne Hamilton deserved to die for that alone.

But this time, with The Cadre's help, his new group, Sons of the Smoky Mountains would succeed. So simple. Find and take the best-looking kids they could and sell them to The Cadre, who had clients offering enormous sums of money for such kids. The amount of money the Sons could make over the next few years was staggering. Money to be used to buy guns and mount an armed revolution. The Sons of the Smoky Mountains would show this country and the world what it meant to be not only a Tennessean but an American. Then America would be America again and it would start in Tennessee.

.   .   .

"ARE THERE other groups like The Cadre operating in this area?" Mac watched Anne pour olive oil into the food processor's feeding tube for the pesto. He'd showered for a long time, letting the hard jets unkink the muscles in his shoulders and back, dissolving the day's tension and making him feel a thousand percent better.

He'd also needed the water's pulsing jets time to wash away the arousal her kiss had caused. This was not the time to get emotionally involved with a BP client. Too much was at stake.

But there was no denying he wanted Anne Hamilton very badly.

He watched the food processor pulverize the basil mixture into paste and she switched it off. "Are there any other groups?" he asked again.

"There have been gangs of one sort or another here for years," Anne said, taking bowls from the warming drawer. "Most are involved in drugs, weapons, and prostitution but I've never heard anything about child trafficking or them having The Cadre's power. Is the pasta ready?"

"Just now." It was amazing how well they worked together. After he drained the pasta and dished it into bowls, Anne poured the pesto over it and added grated cheese. The salad, breadsticks, and wine were already on the table. They sat and after several minutes of silent enjoyment, Mac asked, "Any of these groups have a special agenda?"

She swirled her fork in the bowl, lips pursed in thought. "There was a group operating on the edge seven years ago but were never identified as a gang or involved with one. They were very conservative and preached returning to traditional values, whatever that meant, but they gave me the impression they were a bunch of dissatisfied bullies. Their mission statement was to help members–men only–improve themselves, physically, spiritually, and emotionally, but their organization was very loose, like too many leaders and not enough regular members to the grunt work."

"What did they call themselves?" Mac refilled their empty wine glasses.

Her light laugh was a comforting sound. The good food and sleep were working a special healing on her. "Bad Ass Boys," she said. "BAB."

Mac was glad he'd not taken a sip of the wine. "Really?" he laughed. "Bad Ass Boys?"

"Oh, yeah." She speared a bite of salad and after eating it, said, "As much as I tried to be objective, I wound up making them look foolish–a bunch of guys wanting to be a badass but not knowing how to pull it off. Some of them wrote a letter to Stanley Harris, demanding I be fired. He, of course, refused, and BAB simply fizzled away."

An uneasy concern crept over Mac's skin. "Do you remember any of the members' names?"

She shrugged. "I'll look it up, but honestly, Mac,

I'd be more worried about a bunch of unhappy first graders than those men. They were very silly. I'm not even sure who their founder or leader was."

"Right," he agreed, making a mental note to look up the story. At this point, he needed to know how many possible enemies Anne Hamilton had made over the years. Instead, he said, "Would you tell me about your mom?"

She sighed and wrapped her hands around her wine glasses. "I'll give you the short version," she said. "When I was fourteen years old and a freshman in high school, my father had a 'religious experience'. Turns out he'd had an affair with a co-worker while they were at a week-long conference. She thought he'd leave us for her, and when he refused, she told my mother who was six months pregnant. Mom miscarried and things went to hell in a handbasket. Instead of taking responsibility for his actions, my loving father claimed Satan tempted him into the affair and became a stern, religious zealot. He pulled my younger brother and sisters out of our mainline church and forced us to attend a very patriarchal, fundamentalist style one that had its own small, private school. I rebelled and he 'disowned' me. Fortunately, a juvenile court judge–and my behavior got that bad–placed me with my mother's sister, Ruth Davis and I lived with her until I was eighteen and started college."

Mac peered into his wineglass, framing his next

question. "Have you had much contact with your family since then?" He was quite sure he would not like her father.

She shrugged. "I've spoken with my mother and siblings a handful of times, but my father and I've not spoken since then and he restricts the amount of contact my mother and brothers have with me. For my mother to call me out of the blue meant something was up, but she said that a neighbor had told her about the accident, and she wanted to be sure I was alright."

Heart aching, Mac stared at her beautiful, sad face. He could not imagine growing up without his siblings. They'd fought like cats and dogs at times, but everyone who knew them knew, you take on one MacFarlane, you take on them all. "What about your sisters?"

"Sometimes," she admitted. "My sisters are six and four years younger than me and they married men from that church who restrict how much contact they have with outsiders My twin brothers just turned seventeen, but they wouldn't dare defy my father. He's determined to keep them away from the 'evil, outside world.'".

"It can be evil," Mac said softly. "Did your mother say anything else?"

"Maybe." She leaned forward, excitement brightening her eyes. "I remembered what Barclee had just told us how The Cadre might be hiding the kids in places the police wouldn't look. My home community is rural and there are any number of places someone could hide or be hidden, so when I asked her if she'd heard anything about local farmers hiring young itinerant laborers, she said, 'Ask Amos.'"

"That was a good idea," Mac praised. "Who's Amos?"

"Amos Tindell is a farmer in my home community of Peaksville and the president of the local co-operative," Anne said. "If there's anything odd happening, Amos will know."

Mac considered everything that had happened today and put down his wine glass. "Do you think Barclee is crazy?"

"He's one of the weirdest people I've ever met," she said. "I don't know if that presentation he gave us was a test or if he *is* crazy. But I've known Pastor Cole for years, but if he trusts Barclee enough to bring him to us, that's good enough for me. Any more questions?"

"Yeah. When do we talk to Amos? I'm assuming we will?"

"Tomorrow," she said. "At Third Friday in Peaksville, two hours northeast of here. It's a monthly farmers' market that brings in people from several counties. But we'll need to leave early because of the extra traffic coming into Knoxville this weekend. Lots of people like to get here early."

He sipped his wine before asking, "What's happening in Knoxville this weekend?"

Her grin only added to the wine's warmth surging through him. "You're kidding, right? It's the third Saturday of October."

"So?" he said. "What's the big deal about that?"

"The UT vs Alabama football game," she declared. "The Tide is coming to town!"

"WE DON'T LIKE FAILURE, FRANKLIN." The man behind the desk declared, his voice bouncing off the windowless concrete walls. Except for the small penlight he held, the room was completely dark. "This was a simple enough assignment–grab the Hamilton woman and bring her to me."

"Shit, the bitch pepper sprayed me!" A sweating, shirtless Tyrel Franklin protested as a man in a mask like the one he'd worn earlier, pulled his wrists behind his back and bound them with rope, while the other man stood to the side, knife in hand, waiting. "I had a hold of her arm good and tight–"

"Yet she got away," the voice interrupted. "If you can't do something that simple, you are not to be trusted. Where is Anne Hamilton now?"

"Don't know," Franklin grumbled. His eyes still burned from the pepper spray, and he couldn't smell a thing. "It's not like she gave me her address."

The man with the knife slapped him, hard. Franklin yelped and struggled to break free, but his bonds were too tight, cutting into his wrists' flesh and he had to force himself not to cry out again. "I'm sorry," he whimpered. "I'm sorry."

"You will find her within the next twenty-four hours and let me know where she is. If you fail, you die. You have been warned." The man nodded at the one holding the knife. "Do the L," he commanded.

"No wait! I'll find her!" Franklin cried as he heard the soft 'snick' of a switchblade snapping open. The smell of his sweat was making him gag. "Maybe she'll go back to the newspaper and–"

His screams bounced off the walls as the knife slowly carved the letter L into the flesh of his upper right arm. Something caustic had been rubbed onto the knife's blade and it burned like the flames of hell his preacher grandpappy had warned he would face if he didn't change his ways. The grip on his arms relaxed and his knees buckled, taking him to the floor, sobbing.

"Get him out of here," the man behind the desk ordered. The others did not wait to hear his command issued again. They knew better. Hauling the still sobbing Franklin to his feet, they dragged him from the room and shut the door.

Alone, the man released a volley of curses. He'd been a fool to even try to trust Franklin and couldn't afford to wait twenty-four hours. He'd kill Franklin himself and get someone else to find Anne Hamilton. As much as he would like to kill her himself, someone else had demanded that pleasure.

She'd made BAB look like fools seven years ago with her article, dissolving their plans for a better, stronger Tennessee like sugar in hot tea before they took their mission to the next level. Anne Hamilton deserved to die for that alone.

But this time, with The Cadre's help, his new group, Sons of the Smoky Mountains would succeed. So simple. Find and take the best-looking kids they could and sell them to The Cadre, who had clients offering enormous sums of money for such kids. The amount of money the Sons could make over the next few years was staggering. Money to be used to buy guns and mount an armed revolution. The Sons of the Smoky Mountains would show this country and the world what it meant to be not only a Tennessean but an American. Then America would be America again and it would start in Tennessee.

"ARE THERE other groups like The Cadre operating in this area?" Mac watched Anne pour olive oil into the food processor's feeding tube for the pesto. He'd showered for a long time, letting the hard jets unkink the muscles in his shoulders and back, dissolving the day's tension and making him feel a thousand percent better.

He'd also needed the water's pulsing jets time to wash away the arousal her kiss had caused. This was not the time to get emotionally involved with a BP client. Too much was at stake.

But there was no denying he wanted Anne Hamilton very badly.

He watched the food processor pulverize the basil mixture into paste and she switched it off. "Are there any other groups?" he asked again.

"There have been gangs of one sort or another here for years," Anne said, taking bowls from the warming drawer. "Most are involved in drugs, weapons, and prostitution but I've never heard anything about child trafficking or them having The Cadre's power. Is the pasta ready?"

"Just now." It was amazing how well they worked together. After he drained the pasta and dished it into bowls, Anne poured the pesto over it and added grated cheese. The salad, breadsticks, and wine were already on the table. They sat and after several minutes of silent enjoyment, Mac asked, "Any of these groups have a special agenda?"

She swirled her fork in the bowl, lips pursed in thought. "There was a group operating on the edge seven years ago but were never identified as a gang or involved with one. They were very conservative and preached returning to traditional values, whatever that meant, but they gave me the impression they were a bunch of dissatisfied bullies. Their mission statement was to help members–men only–improve themselves, physically, spiritually, and emotionally, but their organization was very loose, like too many leaders and not enough regular members to the grunt work."

"What did they call themselves?" Mac refilled their empty wine glasses.

Her light laugh was a comforting sound. The good food and sleep were working a special healing on her. "Bad Ass Boys," she said. "BAB."

Mac was glad he'd not taken a sip of the wine. "Really?" he laughed. "Bad Ass Boys?"

"Oh, yeah." She speared a bite of salad and after eating it, said, "As much as I tried to be objective, I wound up making them look foolish–a bunch of guys wanting to be a badass but not knowing how to pull it off. Some of them wrote a letter to Stanley Harris, demanding I be fired. He, of course, refused, and BAB simply fizzled away."

An uneasy concern crept over Mac's skin. "Do you remember any of the members' names?"

She shrugged. "I'll look it up, but honestly, Mac, I'd be more worried about a bunch of unhappy first graders than those men. They were very silly. I'm not even sure who their founder or leader was."

"Right," he agreed, making a mental note to look up the story. At this point, he needed to know how many possible enemies Anne Hamilton had made over the years. Instead, he said, "Would you tell me about your mom?"

She sighed and wrapped her hands around her wine glasses. "I'll give you the short version," she said. "When I was fourteen years old and a freshman in high school, my father had a 'religious experience'. Turns out he'd had an affair with a co-worker while they were at a week-long conference. She thought he'd leave us for her, and when he refused, she told my mother who was six months pregnant. Mom miscarried and things went to hell in a handbasket. Instead of taking responsibility for his actions, my loving father claimed Satan tempted him into the affair and became a stern, religious zealot. He pulled my younger brother and sisters out of our mainline church and forced us to attend a very patriarchal, fundamentalist style one that had its own small, private school. I rebelled and he 'disowned' me. Fortunately, a juvenile court judge–and my behavior got that bad–placed me with my mother's sister, Ruth Davis and I lived with her until I was eighteen and started college."

Mac peered into his wineglass, framing his next question. "Have you had much contact with your family since then?" He was quite sure he would not like her father.

She shrugged. "I've spoken with my mother and siblings a handful of times, but my father and I've not spoken since then and he restricts the amount of contact my mother and brothers have with me. For my mother to call me out of the blue meant something was up, but she said that a neighbor had told her about the accident, and she wanted to be sure I was alright."

Heart aching, Mac stared at her beautiful, sad face. He could not imagine growing up without his siblings. They'd fought like cats and dogs at times, but everyone who knew them knew, you take on one MacFarlane, you take on them all. "What about your sisters?"

"Sometimes," she admitted. "My sisters are six and four years younger than me and they married men from that church who restrict how much contact they have with outsiders My twin brothers just turned seventeen, but they wouldn't dare defy my father. He's determined to keep them away from the 'evil, outside world.'".

"It can be evil," Mac said softly. "Did your mother say anything else?"

"Maybe." She leaned forward, excitement brightening her eyes. "I remembered what Barclee had just told us how The Cadre might be hiding the kids in places the police wouldn't look. My home community is rural and there are any number of places someone could hide or be hidden, so when I asked her if she'd heard anything about local farmers hiring young itinerant laborers, she said, 'Ask Amos.'"

"That was a good idea," Mac praised. "Who's Amos?"

"Amos Tindell is a farmer in my home community of Peaksville and the president of the local cooperative," Anne said. "If there's anything odd happening, Amos will know."

Mac considered everything that had happened today and put down his wine glass. "Do you think Barclee is crazy?"

"He's one of the weirdest people I've ever met," she said. "I don't know if that presentation he gave us was a test or if he *is* crazy. But I've known Pastor Cole for years, but if he trusts Barclee enough to bring him to us, that's good enough for me. Any more questions?"

"Yeah. When do we talk to Amos? I'm assuming we will?"

"Tomorrow," she said. "At Third Friday in Peaksville, two hours northeast of here. It's a monthly farmers' market that brings in people from several counties. But we'll need to leave early because of the extra traffic coming into Knoxville this weekend. Lots of people like to get here early."

He sipped his wine before asking, "What's happening in Knoxville this weekend?"

Her grin only added to the wine's warmth

surging through him. "You're kidding, right? It's the third Saturday of October."

"So?" he said. "What's the big deal about that?"

"The UT vs Alabama football game," she declared. "The Tide is coming to town!"

CHAPTER 10

Friday Morning

"I GUESS I could have just called Amos," Anne said. "But it's been ages since I've gone to Third Friday. And when I'm trying to learn things, it's always better to talk to people face to face."

"Ever the reporter," Mac said. They'd decided to take his truck largely because he felt better driving his vehicle. "Will it be crowded?"

"More so than usual," Anne said. "People driving in for the football game like to stop and shop there before they head to Knoxville. After Christmas, it's the busiest Third Friday of the year."

And maybe the perfect place for someone coming after you to hide. Mac's gaze flickered to the side mirror, then the rearview. They'd met with Hank

Patterson via Zoom before leaving Townsend. After hearing of their plans, he promised to have BP members present at Third Friday, just in case. Griff would follow them there and back in a plain black sedan. And since *Ramsey's* security system was up and running, they were to return there when they'd finished for the day. After Anne's attempted kidnapping, being as close to KPD made sense, and they'd stowed her suitcase in the back. Mac already had clothing at *Ramsey's*. Returning to Anne's home was still not an option, but she assured Hank she had plenty to wear. All in all, they should be reasonably safe.

Reasonably. Mac hoped that was enough.

Now, coffees in the cupholders, they were headed to Peaksville, the community where Anne grew up and that straddled two counties northeast of Knoxville. It was a perfect October day, kissed with warmth but with a touch of fall crispness. The trees lining the climbing roads blazed with gold, russet, and copper leaves, lending a special glow to the morning and Mac felt like they were driving through an enchanted forest. Once out of them, they passed well-tended fields that stretched out for acres, the equally well-kept barns and homes adding their beauty to the landscape.

"You're quiet all of a sudden," Anne said. "What are you thinking?"

"About how I'm going to see the place where

you grew up." Mac forced his caution aside and gave her a broad wink. "I found your online biography last night after you went to bed. I was curious about your career after you said you'd won *Excelsior*'s writing contest when you were in high school. I was impressed."

"Curious about me, were you?" Anne asked. Yesterday's frustration and anger between them were gone, and a friendly camaraderie had taken its place. Mac preferred that. In her jeans, UT sweatshirt, vest, and minimal make-up, she was gorgeous.

"Let's see." He frowned in mock concentration. "Graduated high school with lots of college credits due to a bunch of AP courses and with one of the highest GPAs *ever,* from that school. Awarded a full scholarship to UT–that's Tennessee, not Texas. Double major in journalism and political science, editor of the university paper, and graduated Phi Beta Kappa and summa cum laude. Oh, yeah. Did summer internships at *The New York Times, The Washington Post*, and *The Times of London* when you were in college, with the cherry on top being five years ago, you became the youngest winner of the Dixon Award for Excellence in Journalism. Did they leave anything out?"

"Did it mention I can play Beethoven's *Ode to Joy* on the kazoo?"

He caught her grin from the corner of his eye. "No. Can you? How well?"

"Badly," she laughed. "Very badly. Look for the sign that says, "Farmer's Market up ahead and turn right."

The dirt road leading to the parking area was long and winding, but Mac could see rows and rows of cars, campers, RVs, and trucks lined up ahead. Even with the windows rolled up, the scents of popcorn and caramel apples mingled with roasting meats and biscuits curled through the windows. "Time," he announced as he pulled the truck into a space, "for "second breakfast."

"My sentiments exactly," she agreed as they got out of the truck. "Let me show you around while we find Amos."

Out of habit, Mac moved his gaze to scan the area surrounding them. There looked to be hundreds of booths, food trucks, and pop-up tents selling all kinds of things while people of all ages were milling about, 'meeting and greeting.' But there were no obvious places for someone to hide and Mac let down his guard ever so slightly. "Does this happen every Third Friday?" he asked.

"Hence the name," she said. "It starts in the early spring and continues until the third Friday in December. That one is my favorite because of all the beautiful Christmas gifts, crafts, and ornaments. Not to mention the food."

"Hey Anne!" a white-haired woman in an old-fashioned apron called and waved. "Who's that tall drink of water you've got with you?"

"See?" Mac winked. "Someone knows what that means."

"Hush," Anne scolded but she was smiling as the woman came toward them.

For the next hour, Anne introduced him to everyone who called out to her as her friend, Lt. Keith MacFarlane, retired USMC. To his delight and surprise, everyone shook his hand or kissed his cheek, thanked him "for his service", and offered him something to eat or a "small gift" from their booths. Anne had to buy a woven basket to put in everything. He was gratified but also humbled. After all, he'd only done what Marines do. Their jobs.

And as he watched her interact with people who knew her very well, he was pleased by her down-to-earth manner and geniuses. Despite her sleek grooming and fashion sense, she had not "gotten above her raising" as his father's mother would have said. He was becoming more and more attracted to her and it had nothing to do with last night's kiss.

Don't be an idiot, McFarlane. People don't fall in love within days with people they've just met.

But he was.

"This is second breakfast times two," he said,

putting a small box of scones in Anne's basket. "Are people around here always so friendly to strangers? Or is it because I'm with you? Everyone around here certainly seems to know you."

Her smile was slow as if she was considering her answer. "Maybe both," she said. "Do you see a large red and white pop-up tent anywhere? Amos always uses one."

"I do," Mac said. "Tall drinks of water come in handy, don't they? Especially when they can see over everyone else."

"Are all Scots as silly as you?" she asked, weaving her way through the crowd lining the wide paths between the booths and tents and he fought the urge to take her hand. Her grandmother's salve had done wonders for his skinned fingers.

"Not silly, lass," he told her, letting his father's accent come through again. "But it's a great sense of humor we have. Gets us through the cold, Highland winters, don't you know."

"Oh, my goodness," she sighed. "Cold highland winters. What next?"

"Anne!" A smiling man wearing overalls and a striped shirt was striding their way, waving a straw hat. "Welcome to Third Friday!"

"Amos!" She smiled and returned the man's welcoming embrace. After introducing Mac, she said, "I've got some odd questions for you, but my mother said you might know."

"Let's go to my booth," Amos suggested. "Bit more private. My son can handle any sales while we talk."

They stopped at another booth selling coffee before going to his tent just past a stage-like platform, with standing American flags running around the back. Outside Amos' tent an impressive offering of fall vegetables-squashes, turnips, greens-were neatly stacked and bagged. Business was good and Amos gave a thumbs up to a younger version of himself who was loading the produce into offered sacks. "We encourage folks to bring their tote bags," he explained, leading them to a small table in a corner. "We like being as earth-friendly as we can."

They sat over coffee and some of the scones they'd bought, Mac listened to Anne and Amos chat about community happenings and events. The atmosphere between them was friendly and he was again amazed at her down-to-earth attitude. She may have achieved a measure of success, but she hadn't forgotten where she'd come from, and he liked that about her.

He was liking her more and more and his heart and head were going to be at war about this. She was a BP client and he sure as hell didn't need to put his future work with them in danger.

After about half an hour of conversation, Amos

put his cup on the table and sat back. "Now, Anne. How can I help you?"

She needed no further encouragement. "Has anyone new moved into the area in the last few months or bought property? Someone who might need to hire laborers, especially young laborers?"

The farmer thought. "Someone bought the old Dudley place 'round April," he said after a minute. "But not for farming. A teens' advocacy group called Tomorrow Morning, is opening a treatment center sometime next year. I went to a town meeting over the summer where some of their staff described their program and then checked them out. They seemed legitimate and didn't take kids with criminal backgrounds, so a lot of folks were relieved by that. I've seen some people painting the buildings recently, but nothing seemed suspicious. Is there something going on that I need to know about?"

Her smile was pure innocence. "Now why would you think that?"

Amos chuckled. "Local girl who became a top investigative reporter starts asking questions, I get curious." Then his smile vanished. "Does this have anything to do with those six missing kids in Knoxville?"

"I don't know, Amos," she admitted. "Bits of street gossip are saying whoever has the kids might have them stashed somewhere the police wouldn't know or have reason to look. Peaksville is so rural, that it would be the perfect place to do something like that, but I have no reason to believe it. But if anything, odd was going on, you would know."

A burst of taped patriotic music interrupted her, and they turned to see a man mounting the stage filled with standing American flags. Some people cheered, and the man waved in response. More people clustered around the stage and as the music faded, the man approached a standing microphone and the people's cheering faded. As if of one mind, Anne and Mac rose and walked towards the front of the tent, but halfway there, she put her hand on Mac's arm. "Wait," she whispered. "I don't want him to see us."

"Morning, folks," the man began. "It's a great day for Third Friday. Most of you know me, or hope you do since my paternal grandparents grew up here and got their start in business here. I'm Robert H. Carsen–"

People cheered again and he smiled a practiced smile. In his well-tailored suit, flashing white teeth, and perfect hair, he looked every inch the billionaire entrepreneur that he was. He waved them to silence and continued.

"It's a bit early to make an official announcement, but with the holidays coming on, I wanted to get an early start. I'm here today to announce my plans for running for governor of this great state at the next election!"

More cheering, but beside Mac, both Anne and Amos were frowning. They clearly did not like Carsen and Mac's curiosity clicked open. He'd only known Anne a few days, but already he was coming to know her body language and the set of her shoulders told him she had a damn good reason not to like the man on the stage and he wondered why.

"So, I'm gonna be walking among you today, and listening to what you think needs to happen in our great state, what we need to change, and what we need to do to protect our children!" Carsen's voice rose and he pumped the air with his fist.

More cheering, and Anne touched Mac's arm again. "I think we should quietly slide away," she murmured. "He might be able to see you, Mac, tall as you are, but I don't want him to see me. Amos, you have my number. Would you text me if you hear anything?"

"Count on it," Amos said. He gave her a thoughtful look, then said, "I'm going to take another look at that program over at the Dudley place. Probably means nothing, but it never hurts to be sure. Good to have met you, Lt. MacFarlane. Take care of her. She's precious to us."

"Count on it," Mac echoed as Anne tugged on his sleeve. Her pace as they headed back to the truck was brisk, suggesting she wanted to get the hell out of there as quickly as possible. Once they were back on the road, Mac said, "Would you mind telling me what that was all about? What's your beef with Robert H. Carsen or rather, what's his beef with you?"

She shrugged and moved the basket from the seat to the floor. "I wrote about him when I first started working at *Excelsior*. He was running for re-election on the School Board, and I was assigned to do a story on him. He wanted to introduce strict dress codes and cut funding to afterschool programs for at-risk youth. My story was hardly flattering, but he still won his election. To say he was unhappy with me was an understatement."

"Wasn't *How to Win Friends and Influence People* required reading for you in college?" Mac teased. "First you insult those guys from BAB and then a politician in the making. What does Carsen do when he's not stumping for office?"

"He's an entrepreneur," she said. "His wife's family owns a chain of high-end restaurants all over the state. It's practically an empire. Very pricey, very chic. Carlsen's grandfather started a chain of dollar-type stores years ago, and our would-be politician sold them for a huge profit. He has his fingers in many pies, or so my friends who write about the local business community tell me."

"And you don't like him." Mac stared at an SUV

in the rear-view mirror. It and several other vehicles had left when they did, but now it was the only one behind them and he had a creeping suspicion they were being followed and not by a BP member. Where the hell was Griff?

Her gaze shifted from a study of the passing landscape to his face. "No," she said simply. "He's pompous, narrow-minded, elitist and condescending."

"Only that?" Mac teased.

"I'm sure there's more," she said, and her grin made his heart turn over. "At least we found out there's not much chance of the missing kids being hidden in this area. But if anything changes, Amos will let me know."

"Uh-huh." Mac accelerated ever so slightly, and their companion did the same. When he slowed, it matched their speed. This was more than someone practicing safe driving.

"What is it?" A note of caution entered Anne's voice.

"I think someone is following us," he said. "And I don't think it's BP. Don't turn around."

"What are they driving?" She craned her head as if to look out the rear-view window, but his hand on her arm stopped her.

"I said, don't turn around," he ordered. "It's a red Honda SUV. I noticed some guy who always seemed to be hovering around us when we were visiting the booths. If it weren't so crowded, I'd have said something to him."

The SUV's horn honked, and as it eased past them. Mac had just enough time to see a man in a baseball cap holding up a small American flag and give him a thumbs up. It sped past them, and Mac quickly memorized the license plate number. TN RKB 2244.

"There, you see?" Anne said. "He must have heard me introduce you as a Marine and was too shy to say thank you in person."

"Maybe," he said. "But being a Marine taught me one thing, it's to trust your instincts and mine tell me someone was watching us the entire time we were at Third Friday. I see a convenience market up ahead. Let's stop for gas."

Inside, the store was crowded, and more than one voice was raised about the traffic on the Inter-state into Knoxville. "Damn near bumper to bumper, and now we have to stop at all these little hick places," a woman proclaimed loudly. "And now they're calling for rain."

Back on the road, Mac said, "Is it really going to be bumper to bumper back to Knoxville or is there another way to go?"

"I can show you a different route," Anne said. "The only problem is sometimes cell coverage drops so if we need help, it might be hard to call for it. It will take longer but the scenery is fabulous."

A desire to be alone with her for as long as he could nearly overwhelm Mac, but he managed to laugh and say, "Well, then my bonnie lassie, show me the way. If we find a picnic table, we can stop and eat all the food we bought. One scone is hardly enough food to keep a man or a lass on their feet."

Anne pulled out her phone and hit some buttons. "Checking the traffic," she said. "Yep, that woman was right. Back-to-back on the interstate due to several rear-enders. My way will definitely be quicker."

The afternoon turned magical. Even the overcast sky didn't darken their moods, and Mac pushed aside any worry about losing cell coverage. They sang classic rock songs, playfully argued about their favorite sports teams, and shared their favorite Christmas traditions, including food. The rain didn't fall, so they were able to enjoy a picnic at a roadside park.

It was after five o'clock and getting dark when they finally pulled out onto the interstate and were met with a line of evenly flowing traffic. "Looks like the fender-benders were cleared up," Anne said, the relief apparent in her voice. "I guess I better check my messages."

"It was nice to take a break from all of this, wasn't it?" Mac asked softly. "It's been almost non-stop since we met."

She turned to him, her face luminous in the

cab's semi-darkness. "It was a beautiful day," she answered, her voice equally soft.

Then she took out her phone, scanned the screen, and sighed. "We missed a call from Sergeant Miller a half hour ago," she announced. "Let's see what's up." She punched accept and put it on speaker. "Good evening, Sergeant Miller," she greeted. "Do you have news for us? Good news, I hope."

"Is Lt. MacFarlane with you?" Tension radiated through Grant Miller's usually calm voice. "Are you both safe, Ms. Hamilton?"

"I am and we are," Mac answered. "We're on our way back to Knoxville from Third Friday. Is something wrong?"

"Depends on how you look at it," Miller replied.

"Oh dear," Anne sighed and leaned against the door. Worry pulled her pretty mouth into a frown. "This sounds like bad news."

"You could say that," Miller continued. "A woman found a man's naked body early this afternoon in the alley running behind *Excelsior* with the initials LS carved into his chest. She wants to talk to you and said to tell you, 'Barclee says to talk to Tall Man and Pretty Writer Lady. They help you.' I'm guessing that means you two."

"LS," Mac repeated, pushing down on the accelerator. "Son of a bitch. Los Silenciosos. The Cadre."

CHAPTER 11

"Her working name is Cassie Girl," Miller said. "Real name is Cassandra Douglas, aged twenty-seven, or so she says. I would add ten years to that, but that's just my observation. She's been in town about a year, arrested once for solicitation, but nothing else. Officer Matt Collins heard her screaming at about four o'clock this afternoon and found her standing over the victim's naked body in the alley running behind *Excelsior* next to the garbage bins. We're waiting on the coroner's report, but Collins said it looked like someone broke his neck. And of course, those initials carved on his chest. Bit of nasty work."

"The garbage is picked up at *Excelsior* on Thursday morning," Anne said. "And then not again until Saturday, but I'm not sure how many people might wander through that alley during the day. I wonder how long the body was there."

"Collins reported the body was stiff to his touch, so he might have been killed last night or early this morning and dumped there when no one was around," Miller described. "She's calmer now, but she was spooked when we brought her in." He chuckled and added, "Though I'm sure seeing naked bodies isn't new to her."

"But how often does she see dead ones with initials carved in their chest?" Mac asked and Miller nodded.

Anne studied the woman sitting at the table in the interview room behind the one-way glass. Her bright, bleached blonde beehive hairdo was coming undone, and her raddled make-up gave her face a hard, angry look. Her too-large denim jacket hung over a low-cut black dress and her restless fingers wandered between playing with her dangling earrings and numerous necklaces.

But her dark-eyed gaze, fixed on the glass, was sad and tired and Anne wondered how she had come to this life. "It's okay for us to talk to her?" she asked.

Miller shrugged. "Like I said, she asked for the two of you. There have been several bar fights downtown starting late last night and again this afternoon pre-game special that has kept us busy. She said she was tired and hungry, so we got her a meal and let her sleep until right before I called you. She's not charged with anything, so I guess she'll eventually call her old man to come get her."

"Well, let's see what Miss Cassandra Douglas wants with us," Anne suggested.

With its long, metal table and battered matching chairs, the cold, overly bright room was right off the set of a crime show. Cassie jerked as they entered, and her eyes widened. "Holy shit," she breathed out, staring up at Mac. "Barclee was right. You are a tall man." Shifting her regard to Anne, she said, "I know who you are. You're that hotshot reporter. I saw you on TV once."

"That's right," Anne said as they sat. "I'm Anne Hamilton from *Excelsior*. This is Mac. We're doing a story about crime in the area and hope you will tell us what happened this morning." She left out who Mac was. Let Cassie think he was a reporter too. "Was there a reason you were in the alley behind *Excelsior* this afternoon?"

"If you're doing a story, aren't you going to take notes or something?" Cassie asked petulantly. "And I don't want this recorded, you know what I mean?"

"Of course," Anne agreed. She took an old-fashioned stenographer's notebook and pen from her purse and slid them over to Mac. From the corner of her eye, she could see him suppress a grin as he opened the pad and put pen to paper.

"A woman in charge," Cassie said. "I like that."

"Me too," Anne agreed. "Can you please tell us what happened this morning?"

"I hope this isn't gonna take too long," she said, returning suddenly nervous hands to explore her necklaces again. "My old man is gonna be pissed if I'm not out earning his living."

"We'll be quick," Anne promised. "You told the police that Barclee told you to ask for us. Where's Barclee now?"

Cassie shrugged. "Don't know," she admitted. "The man's like smoke. Comes and goes and nobody knows, but if he wants to find you, he will. I guess you could say he's a friend. Anyway, he heard me screaming this afternoon and came running. Don't know where he came from, but then I never do. He told me to tell the cops to find you and then took off. But I owe him a favor, so I'll talk to you."

"I wonder what kind of favor," Mac murmured, taking down Cassie's account. Looking up, he asked, "Why were you in the alley running behind *Excelsior?* Seems an odd place to be on a Friday afternoon."

A blush stained Cassie's cheek. "Sometimes I find copies of yesterday's newspapers there near the garbage cans," she said defensively. "I like to read the gardening section when I get my coffee from the food trucks. So, when I finished my last job this afternoon–and I ain't tell you who it was–I went to see if any papers there and that's when I found the body."

She shuddered and the hard, blasé demeanor fell away. "He was naked, you know? Not that bothers me, but it was those initials carved on his chest, big and bloody and raw that started me screaming and I realized he was dead."

Recalling Henry's description of what The Cadre's initiates were made to do, Anne made sure her voice was steady before she asked, "What initials?"

"L. S.," Cassie said. "And before you go asking if they were his initials, they weren't. Tyrel could be a prick at times, but he didn't deserve that."

"You know who he was?" Anne exchanged glances with Mac.

"Yeah, Tyrel Franklin." Cassie's mouth pulled to the side. "He's a-was-a two-bit wanna-be-enforcer. You know, rough people up for hire. He was trying to start his stable but we girls just laughed at him. But here lately–"

Fear wiped the color from her face, leaving it pale beneath the makeup, and she lowered her voice as if the walls could hear them. "Tyrel was bragging about how he was working for that new gang in town that's been taking over the other gangs' territory, making them mad as spit but too scared to do anything to stop them. They're calling them 'the scary ones,' 'cause they're as scary and sneaky as a devil out of hell. Folks say you'd never see them coming until they were in your face."

Los Silenciosos, Anne thought. Silent ones. Close enough to 'scary ones.' Beside her, Mac made more notes.

"Any talk about what the scary ones are up to?" Mac asked, and Anne heard the gentleness in his voice. "Guns, drugs, taking a fellow's stable from him?"

Her eyes explored his expression and after a moment, she nodded. "Kids," she said. "Word is they've snatched a bunch of 'em and are gonna send 'em to Atlanta."

Her heart banging against her ribs made breathing difficult but Anne managed to inhale silently and ask, "You mean like those kids whose pictures are up everywhere? Like that latest girl– what's her name, Mac?"

Mac's furrowed eyebrows gave the impression he was trying to remember. "Katie Johnson," he said at last.

She nodded. "And what does this group plan to do with these kids when they get to Atlanta?" Anne asked. *We're getting close. Hang on Katie, wherever you are.*

"Sell them to a bunch of short eyes."

"You mean pedophiles," Mac said. " 'Short eyes' is what they're called in prison, right?"

"Yeah," Cassie grimaced. "That kind of stuff is sick, you know? Really sick."

"We know," Anne said softly. "This group has a name?"

Cassie's fingers curled into fists. "The Cadre," she whispered. "That's what Henry told me."

Whatever answer Anne was expecting, this wasn't it. "Henry? Henry Cooper?"

"Yeah." A tiny smile lit up Cassie's face. "Henry and me, we had sort of a friend-with-benefits relationship. He knew how to treat a woman right, especially when she wasn't in the sack with him. If my old man Louie was on a bender and threatening to beat my ass, Henry would let me stay with him until the dust settled. He moved around a lot and never told me where it was until I needed it, so Louie wouldn't find us."

He gave me the keys. Anne remembered. *Henry gave me the keys to his place.* Excitement tingled through her fingers. "Do you know the last place Henry lived?"

"Yeah," Cassandra said, and her hands relaxed. "It was a new place, but I was there with him the night before he died."

"Did he seem worried or scared about anything?" Anne was still trying to picture this woman and Henry together but couldn't conjure it.

"Everyone's scared of those guys," Cassie whispered again as if saying 'The Cadre' out loud might bring down some curse. "But Henry had this book where he kept stuff written down. He said it was an appointment book but who knows? Maybe he wrote about them, and they found out, so they killed him. Are you gonna help the police get them?"

"We're going to do our best," Anne said. "He was my friend for a long time."

Cassie's grin made her almost pretty. "Okay, fair is fair. Since I helped you, can you help me get Henry a veteran's funeral?"

Mac put down his pen. "How do you know Henry was a veteran?"

"Because I'm the one who took his dog tags to *Excelsior.*" Tears sparkled in her eyes, and she gestured at Anne. "I remembered you worked there and thought if I brought you the dog tags, you could help to get him a veteran's funeral. Like I said we were together the night before he was killed." She plucked at the jacket's collar and added, "He must have put the dog tags in the pockets before we went to bed. I guess he forgot 'cause he let me borrow this the next morning. I found them later but by then it was too late. He was dead."

She took a suspiciously clean handkerchief from the jacket's pocket and blew her nose. "Called them his good luck charms," she gulped. "Maybe if he'd had them, that damn car wouldn't have run him down and he'd still be alive. But he was a Marine. He needs to be buried with his tribe, ya know?" Worry narrowed her eyes. "You got them, didn't you? His dog tags?"

"We did," Mac said. "And as a Marine and a veteran, I give you my word, we'll get Henry a veteran's funeral."

Cassie's mouth fell open. "You're a veteran?"

Mac rose to his full height and gave her a smart salute. "Lt. Keith MacFarlane, USMC, retired, at your service, Ms. Douglas," he announced. He pulled out his dog tags from under his sweater. "Here's proof if you need it. I kept mine too."

"Ohhh," she sighed. "MacFarlane. That's Scottish, isn't it? Like Douglas."

"Aye, my bonnie lass", his brogue turning rich and rolling and Cassie roared with laughter, erasing the fear from her face.

"You sound just like those guys on *Outlander*," she gasped. "Are you Scottish?"

"On both sides," he said. "I was born and raised here, but I go back there whenever I can. 'Tis a grand place to visit, but you better like rain, 'cause it rains a lot there."

"Let me ask you something," she asked. "Do you Scottish guys really go commando under your kilts?" Her giggle was like a young girl's. "You know, without any–"

"An officer and a gentleman never tell," he

declared solemnly. "So, I'm bound by a code of honor to keep that information a secret."

Cassie laughed again and her gaze gave them once over. "You two hooked up?"

"I'm her bodyguard," Mac said. "No benefits allowed."

"Like in that Whitney Houston movie," she said wistfully. "Kevin Costner sure took care of her, didn't he?"

"He did, and now we're going to take care of you," Mac said, nodding at Anne. "We'll get you a bodyguard and a place to stay since it's not safe for you to go back to Henry's. I'll bet my grandfather's bagpipes someone will think you're there. But if you'll give us his address, we'll go see if there's anything that can help us track down his killer."

"I can do that," she said. With a coy smile, she plucked the pen from Mac's hand, retrieved a card for *Yasmin's Falafel Hut* from the jacket's pocket, and scribbled on the back. "It's not an address," she said, returning the pen and the card. "But this is how to get there. Better take a flashlight 'cause it's dark as a pitch back there. Good place to hide."

"We'll be careful," Anne assured her. "Thank you for your help."

"Okay, but how are you gonna get in?" Cassie asked. "You gonna break in somehow?"

"An officer and a gentleman never tell," Mac repeated, giving her a wink. "But they teach us all kinds of useful stuff in the Marines that come in handy. Contact Officer Miller if you need us and we'll come running."

After assuring Miller they would take care of finding Cassie a safe place to stay, they headed for the front doors. In the distance, they could hear the faint sound of *Rocky Top* being played, a sure sign it was football time in Tennessee.

Outside the station, Anne stared at him. "'My bonnie lassie?' 'My grandfather's bagpipes?' Isn't that laying it on a bit thick?

"Whatever it takes," Mac said. "The question is how to get into Henry's apartment. I don't think I want to add breaking though I've done it before–to my updated resume."

"No need." Anne pulled Henry's keys from her purse and jangled them before him. "These should do the trick."

Mac snatched them out of her hand. "You have keys to Henry's apartment? Why didn't you say something?"

Anne couldn't resist giving him her sauciest smile. "Because you–"

"–didn't ask," he answered, and his sudden grin made her toes curl. "Okay, Miss Hotshot Reporter. Let's go look for Henry's appointment book."

CHAPTER 12

Earlier that evening

ONE GOOD THING *about having hackers on your payroll is that they can get into just about anything.* Scaren stared at the information on the desk. So that black Dodge Ram truck belonged to a former Marine. At least the minion he'd sent to follow Anne Hamilton and her tall friend today had gotten the license tag number right. Lt. Keith MacFarlane, USMC, retired almost two years ago. Scaren's hacker was still trying to learn just what MacFarlane had been doing since then and where he'd been doing it.

But in the meantime, Scaren needed to finalize the plans for getting that extraordinarily beautiful girl here from Charlotte to add to the "pretty six" as he called them to finish the order from that group in Atlanta. When The Cadre paid him the second half of the money for the kids, The Sons of the Smoky Mountains would return the favor and purchase all the guns they needed and could move to the next phase.

But even before that, he would kill Anne Hamilton and Keith MacFarlane both. And he would enjoy doing it.

Because no one stopped Scaren. No one.

"THERE ARE APARTMENTS IN HERE?" Anne asked. "It looks way too creepy for anyone to live here."

Cassie's directions had taken them down several side streets away from the police station, each turning into another until they were making their way through a long trash-strewn alley to an old building with boarded-up windows. An evening rain had started, darkening the sky and eating up what little light was left of the day. Bits of broken glass crunched under their feet and an ominous rustling and squeaking came from the piles of newspapers and smashed, empty Styrofoam take-out boxes.

"But it's a great place to hide if you don't want anyone to come looking for you." Mac coughed against the sour smell of stale coffee grounds, banana peels, and old onion skins piled in a corner. "I just hope it smells better inside. Can you hand me the keys and hold the flashlight please?"

Anne nodded and exchanged the keys from her pocket for the oversized flashlight he held. Holding it steady, she watched as Mac fitted the key to the building's front door.

"You could use this thing as a weapon," Anne commented, appreciating the flashlight's weight. "I can't recall ever seeing one this long."

"BP can do better than that," he said, patting his left shoulder, assured by the touch of the holster and its contents underneath his coat. "You don't think I'd bring you here with just a flashlight for a weapon, do you?"

He almost laughed as she stared at him in open-mouthed surprise. "You have a gun with you?" she hissed. "Really? Why didn't you–"

"I didn't tell you because you didn't ask, but assumed you'd know I would have one," Mac whispered back, unlocking the door. "I've heard that you're kind of smart, don't you know."

"Hush," she hissed, but she was smiling. "Let's get inside."

"I think keeping the lights off–if there are any– will be in our best interest, don't you?" he asked, pushing the door open. "Just in case?"

"Agreed," she said as they stepped inside.

The building's foyer was its nightmare of filth and debris. Broken furniture and a window air conditioner unit lay abandoned, garbage spilled from plastic bags onto the curling linoleum, and piles of newspapers and empty plastic bags were piled into a corner.

"Okay, I was wrong. It smells worse." Mac coughed as they kicked their way through the garbage, unable to avoid stepping in a variety of sticky residue and muck covering the floor. "It's like an open sewer."

"I hope BP has a generous expense account," his companion grumbled, kicking aside a used fast-food bag smeared with what looked to be a mixture of catsup and pickle relish. "These are new sneakers. What is that stuff?"

"Let's not think about it," Mac suggested, as they turned a corner. "Here we are. Door number two." Under the flashlight's gleam, he fitted the second key into the lock, turned the knob, and slowly opened the door. As they crossed the threshold into Henry Cooper's last home, Anne's hand slipped into his, and Mac locked the door behind them.

Unlike the alley and foyer, the large single room was immaculate. No dishes cluttered the sink, no trash littered the floor and the air smelled clean. A small narrow bed was neatly and tightly made, a nightstand and lamp beside it. A loveseat and two chairs made up a seating area, and the wooden floor was swept clean. A small table with two chairs was placed at the end of the kitchen and just past the bedroom area, Mac could see a hall that must lead to the bathroom.

"If I didn't already know Henry Cooper was a Marine, this place would give it away," Mac commented. "Neat, tidy, good use of space. My drill sergeant would have loved him. I'll bet you could bounce a quarter off that bed."

"You can try that before we leave," Anne said. "Let's just see if we can find that ledger."

"You knew Henry," Mac said as he advanced on the lone built-in bookcase, slipping his fingers through the small leather loop at the end of the flashlight and holding it up. "Where would he hide something? Among these books?"

"I don't know," He heard the regret in her voice as she came to stand beside him while he moved the flashlight's beam over the books' spines. "There was so much I didn't know about him and will never know now."

"He trusted you with the information he shared, didn't he?" Mac moved his searching gaze of the books' titles to her face. In the faint glow, her face was luminous and sad. "You're helping to track down Henry Cooper's killer and get him a veteran's funeral. That counts for something. And you're doing a damn good job at it too."

"I am?" Her whispered question started an unexpected longing surging through Mac.

"Word of MacFarlane, a Marine and a Brotherhood Protector," he said solemnly.

Her lips curved into one of the sexiest smiles Mac had ever seen. "In what order would that be?"

"Alphabetical," he said, fighting the urge to pull her into his arms and kiss her silly. "BP, MacFarlane, Marine."

"And how is a woman to be sure such a promise will be kept?"

Oh, what the hell. "Well, sometimes we seal it with a kiss."

He pulled her in his arms and lowered his mouth to hers, savoring the taste of it. Soft and as intoxicating as any whiskey he'd ever tasted. Her quickening breath competed with the roaring in his ears, and he could feel the urgency and longing in her touch as her hands explored his back. It was only the flashlight slipping from his fingers that brought him back to reality and regretfully, he stepped back.

"I think we should talk about this later," he said, picking up the flashlight. "When we're back at *Ramsey's*, maybe."

"I'll go look in the bathroom," she said hastily. "He could have hidden the ledger under some towels."

"Good idea," he said. "I'll look in his nightstand drawers and then look in the refrigerator. I knew someone who kept a copy of their will in the freezer. Here, take the flashlight."

"I have a penlight in my vest pocket," she whispered, stepping away. "I'll be fine."

Stupid, stupid, stupid, MacFarlane. How many times do I have to tell you to get a grip? You got six missing kids, a dead CI, and a woman who's been nearly killed twice since you met her and you're kissing her?

He was thinking of doing a hell of a lot more than kissing her.

Muttering an old Scottish petition for protection against fair damsels, Mac went through the nightstand's three drawers.

They held nothing but changes of neatly rolled underwear socks, and t-shirts. A few simple shirts and jeans hung on a standing clothing rack in a corner, with a pair of boots and a pair of dress shoes underneath it.

"Mac?" Anne's soft voice called. "I think I may have found something."

Crossing the short distance in a few steps, he stopped at the entrance to the bathroom. With its toilet, sink, and shower box, it was hardly big enough for one person and there was no window. Anne was leaning against the shower box door, holding up a bathmat. Pointing the penlight at the floor, she said, "Look at that."

In the glow, Mac saw a handle on what

appeared to be a tiny trapdoor, measuring no more than six inches on either side. "What the fu–"

"I tried to lift it myself," she said apologetically. "I know it's small, but that handle is massively heavy. Care to give it a try?"

"Anything for a lady." He stepped inside, and the tiny space seemed to swallow them, emphasizing their closeness. Her subtle scent invaded his senses again, speeding up his heart. Her jade green eyes gleamed like a jungle cat's and in the flashlight's soft glow, her ebony hair shone like the fur of a panther, soft and inviting, begging to be stroked.

He reached out to do just that. "Has anyone ever told you that you look like a jungle cat?" he asked. It was like touching a bolt of spilled silk, heavy and soft beneath his fingers.

Her smile was warm and inviting and she leaned into him. "Yeah," she whispered, managing to wrap her arms around him and shut off the penlight. "With everything that's happened in the past few days, I sure hope I have nine lives."

"Me too," he whispered and not giving a damn, kissed her again, forcing himself to do it slowly, so he could taste every centimeter of her lips. Sweetness exploded over his mouth again, rich and heady. A soft moan escaped from her throat, and she pressed herself against him so he could feel her heart hammering against his and it was not the closeness of the space that made breathing difficult.

Mac could not recall the last time he'd felt this light-headed.

But then she stepped back and reluctantly, Mac let his arms fall, already missing her warmth. "Wow," was all he could find to say.

"That's the second time we've done that in about ten minutes," she gasped, shoving the penlight into her coat pocket.

"Five," he answered. "But who's counting?"

"I think we do have a lot to talk about when we get back to *Ramsey's*," she said, touching his face. "There'll be plenty enough of time then."

"Agreed," he said. "Let's see what's inside this bad boy."

He knelt and pulled up the door. The space beneath was about twelve inches deep and dust-free, containing only a drawstring bag. He pulled it out and reaching inside, took out a paperbound volume. 'Light please?" he asked.

Under the flashlight's glow, he opened the volume and riffled through pages covered in a series of numbers and letters in different size groupings. "Was Henry a cryptographer?" he asked.

He was more than aware that she'd slipped her arm around his waist. Having her touch him again felt good. More than good.

It felt right.

"I don't know," she said, and again he heard the regret in her voice. "We both liked crossword puzzles and anagrams, and would have contests to see who could finish them first, but something like this? I have no idea."

A rattling at the front door's lock rang loud in the silence. Mac snapped off the flashlight, put a finger to his lips, and pulled his service revolver from his shoulder holster.

"What's that?" Anne whispered.

"The sound of a lock being picked," he hissed as the front door clicked closed. "Call 911 and stay here."

Stepping into the tiny hall separating the bathroom from the living area, he edged himself against the wall. A lone figure turned on the light over the stove, and a faint glow lessened the apartment's darkness. Mac waited and watched.

A heavy-set, dark-haired man opened the refrigerator doors, keeping his back to the room, as he started shoving things around or throwing them on the floor. The silent tread Mac developed over the years came in handy because he was almost upon the intruder when he asked, "Can I help up you find something?"

"Son-of-a-bitch!" The heavy-set man turned, and slammed the refrigerator shut while throwing a large package of frozen chicken at Mac, striking his chest dead center. Mac staggered but regained his footing with the speed of a well-trained Marine and sprang forward to place the barrel of the gun into the man's chest, backing him against a wall.

"I don't like it when people talk that way about my mother," Mac growled. "I think you owe her and me an apology. So, unless you want me to blow you to hell, don't move. Who sent you?"

"Fuck you," the man replied but except for his darting glance, he held still, arms splayed against the wall.

"Such language in front of a lady," Mac chided. Grabbing the man by his coat collar, he shoved him into one of the kitchen chairs and it wobbled under his weight. "Keep your sorry ass where it is."

"Do you need help?" Anne called, the squeaking of her shoes was loud on the wooden floor as she joined him.

"Did you summon the constabulary to this location, my beauty?" Mac should have known she wouldn't stay put. Stanley Harris was right. She was stubborn as hell.

"They're on the way," Anne replied, stopping behind him. "Should we tie him up with these?"

Mac's gaze flickered toward her, and he blinked, not quite sure of what she was holding up. "Are those your pantyhose? You wear pantyhose under jeans?"

"I was cold this morning," she said. "You'd be surprised at how strong they are. You can do the honors while I hold the gun on him. As a Marine, I'll bet you're good at tying knots."

"I usually hate surprises, but I think this might change my mind." Mac kept his attention on the now open-mouthed man. "Do you know how to shoot?"

"I had lots of practice shooting the copperheads that visited my grandmother's vegetable garden in the summer," she said. Giving the man a glare Mac would hate to receive, she said, "And standing this close, it would be awfully hard to miss."

In the distance, sirens faintly wailed, and Mac shook his head. "I think I'll just hang on to Sweet Nell until reinforcements arrive. But if you want to tie him up, I'll make sure he doesn't move. How good are you at tying knots?"

"Top award for it in my senior Girl Scout troop," she boasted. "Can you get him on the floor so I can tie his hands behind his back?"

"I ain't getting on the ground for no bitch," the man snarled, half-rising until Mac shoved the gun's barrel into his chest.

"Call her a bitch again and I may shoot you just for the fun of it," he warned. "Get on the floor and lay on your stomach. Do it very, very slowly."

Before the man could answer, Mac jerked him from the chair, onto the floor, and then his roar of laughter nearly made him lose his grip on his gun as Anne plopped herself on the man's ass, digging her knees into his sides and set about her task with a speed and skill that bordered on scary.

The front door swung open, and Sergeant Grant Miller burst into the room, followed by two other much younger officers as Anne got to her feet. Miller took in the scene and shook his head as he joined them. "I was going to ask if everyone was ok, but it seems you two have the situation well in hand."

"I'd say so," Mac agreed, hauling the tied man upright and shoving him at Miller. "Officer, you may take him away. I think charges of breaking and entering will do to start."

"You got it," a grinning Miller said, taking the man by the arm. "Let's go, sir. You have the–"

But the bound man had other ideas. With an adrenaline-soaked fury, he roared, broke free from Miller, and pivoted to deliver a perfect roundhouse kick against Mac's left knee, sending him to the floor. Glad for his own supply of curses–all in Gaelic so the lady with them wouldn't be offended–Mac sank to the floor, curling into a ball, and then rolled onto his side.

Still raging, his assailant charged at Anne, pushing her against the refrigerator. Mac's heart surged at her gasp, and he struggled to stand, only to have his legs crumple beneath him, sending him back to the floor.

But then he had the satisfaction of watching her

leap toward their assailant like the panther she was and swipe her perfectly manicured fingernails across the side of his face, followed by her smashing the flashlight against his nose in a two-handed grip. His blood shot out, spattering her face and sweatshirt. Never had the sound of bone and cartilage crunching against metal sounded so good to Mac. He would have cheered but he was having trouble breathing from the pain.

The man screamed and nearly joined Mac on the floor, but Miller yanked him up and shoved him at the two rooted-to-the-spot officers. "Get his sorry ass out of here but take him to the closest hospital before you take him downtown."

"Yes, Sergeant Miller," one answered, going to help his partner haul away the still-moaning man while reciting his Miranda rights. After watching them go, Miller turned his narrow-eyed gaze on them. "I think we need an ambulance," he announced as Anne joined Mac on the floor.

"No," Mac groaned. "I'm fine. I've trained as an EMT and medic. I'm fine."

"You are not," Anne argued. "I don't think you're going to be able to walk anywhere, even if we did park just around the corner. And there's no way you're going to be able to drive. I'll call Griff. We won't need an ambulance, Sergeant Miller."

"Hate to argue with a lady, but I'm calling one anyway," Miller declared, pulling on a pair of latex gloves and retrieving the flashlight while Anne placed her call. "You can fight it out with the EMTs when they get here. I'll take this in to see if some skin as well as blood was left on it. Ms. Hamilton, may I please have your sweatshirt?"

"Sure thing," she said, pulling the stained garment over her head and passing it to him. To Mac's great relief, she wore a Lady Vols t-shirt underneath. "What a night," he murmured.

"Thanks," Miller said. "I'll have this back to you as soon as possible." He left, phone in hand, ordering an ambulance to their location. A chilling breeze swept through the still-open front door and beneath his jacket, Mac shivered.

"Hurt much?" Anne asked sympathetically, gently tugging him into a sitting position.

"Naw, I love having my knee smashed by steel-toed boots," Mac grimaced. "I'd ask you to go dancing at Cotton-Eyed Joe's, but I don't think I could manage more than a slow line dance and you've got blood all over your coat, which is against their dress code. They're probably closed by now anyway."

"Don't be a smart ass," she chided, chucking him gently on the chin.

"Remind me to not piss you off the next time you're holding a flashlight." Mac managed to take a handkerchief from his jeans pocket and gently wipe the blood from her face while still concentrating on his breathing. "That was a hell of a swing," he gasped. "That punk will remember the sound of his bones shattering for a long time. I wonder how much skin and blood the flashlight picked up."

"I don't know about that, but we'll have this." She held up her hands. "I think I got enough of it under my nails to get us a DNA sample. Between it and his blood on my sweatshirt, I am going to ask BP to pay for having it dry-cleaned as well as replace my shoes- we should have enough to see if he's in any of those databases they always talk about on the TV crime shows."

"You scratched him too?" Mac gritted his teeth as the pain surged through his knee. "I thought I'd dreamed of seeing that."

She grinned. "Like the jungle cat, I am."

"Good kitty," he whispered, sinking against her as the roar of the ambulance's siren announced its arrival. "That's a good kitty."

CHAPTER 13

"This place is amazing," Anne praised as she walked around the spacious front room of the suite at *Ramsey's.* She'd heard a lot about the beauty of the boutique hotel's simple, elegant beauty, but this was like something out of a design magazine. She'd need to take out a small loan just to have lunch here. "The whole fifth floor really belongs to BP?" she asked, returning to the office with its impressive computer system.

"After our case in Knoxville this past spring, Hank thought it would be a good idea to have a base here, so he bought it," Mac explained, his face a mask of pure misery. Having heard his grunts of pain from one of the bedrooms, Anne guessed removing his jeans and boots was more than a little bit painful. Now, in a t-shirt and sweatpants, his injured leg propped on a hassock in front of one of the sofas, and his hair mussed from taking off his sweater, he looked like a grumpy, bearded bear pulled out of hibernation too early.

A sexy bear she would love to curl up with. "You were saying, Dr. Jones?" she asked of the short, square man who was packing up his medical bag.

"You need to stay off your feet for at least twenty-four hours, if not longer, MacFarlane," Abel Jones, MD, warned "I can guarantee you that you're not going to feel like standing for more than a few minutes. I still think you should have let the ambulance take you to a local ER."

Mac had refused to go anywhere but *Ramsey's* after the ambulance arrived at Henry's place. The EMTs did a once-over and said he'd probably live. Anne and Griff had managed to pack him into the back of Griff's Honda–his own car for a change–and driven the short distance back to *Ramsey's* and called Dr. Jones. While waiting for him, Anne had showered and changed into clean jeans and a sweater but left off her shoes. This carpet felt too good to miss. After braiding her hair, she stuck the folding brush/comb in her back jeans pocket and rolled her other clothes into a towel in case Sergeant Miller needed them for DNA samples as well.

"Why go to the ER on a Friday night where I'd be waiting for hours or maybe even days to be seen for a minor injury instead of coming here and calling you, Dr. Jones?" Mac groused. "You said nothing was broken or shattered, just badly bruised. Besides, I trained as a medic and worked as an EMT before I joined the Marines, so I think I would know if I needed an ER, and I don't."

"At least *Ramsey's* had a wheelchair," Griff said. "There's no way you could have hobbled into the hotel to the elevator, even with Anne and me holding you up."

Mac scowled again and Anne quickly changed the subject. "Hopefully there was enough blood on my sweatshirt and under my fingernails to get a DNA sample." Sergeant Miller had stayed long enough to take care of that while the EMTs tried to talk Mac into going to the ER and Jones had just cleaned her nails and bagged what was under them.

"I've always wondered how women with finger-nails like yours could get any work done," Jones joked as he headed for the suite's front door. "Mac-Farlane, I've left some painkillers for you. I think you're going to need them. But you need to get some rest. Call me if you need me."

"I'm not sleepy," Mac grumped. "And I prefer my painkillers in the liquid form of twelve-year-old scotch, thank you very much."

"I'll go with you, Doc," Griff said, picking up his coat from a chair. "Time to start looking at Henry

Cooper's ledger. As Jones said, call me if you need me."

The men exited the suite and Anne went to perch on the arm of one of the room's sofas and stare at Mac. "Other than your knee hurting like hell, why are you so cranky?"

"Other than not anticipating that bastard's move and being put out of commission, not to mention letting you get hurt?" Mac snapped. "Gee, I don't know. Don't you remember what Cassie said? The kids are going to be moved in the next forty-eight hours, maybe less and I can barely get on clean clothes, much less stand for any length of time. Don't you get it? I failed kids again. *Again.* Just like I failed the Sayyid children. I've fucked this up just like I did back then. I've–"

"You listen to me, 'Scotty,'" Anne shouted, advancing on him. Placing her hands on the chair's arms, she leaned in. "You haven't fucked up anything! Anyone would be stopped by a round-house kick delivered in steel-toed boots! Yeah, he shoved me into the refrigerator, but I had worse playing with my younger brothers. I'm not hurt. You've saved my ass twice since we met, so will you drop the Marine or Highland pride or self-pity or whatever it is and get a grip? You haven't failed. If you hadn't come along, I'd still be spinning my wheels about all of this. I might even be dead. We're going to find those kids. *You haven't failed.*"

Tension rippled through the room, building like a summer storm charging the air. The heaviness grew and grew until Anne thought it would break open and release the sparking desire between them. For a moment, she thought she saw the sheen of relieved tears in Mac's eyes, and she wondered if he could hear the roaring of her heart, so loud was the sound in her own ears.

Then he blinked hard and gave her a wan smile. "Ah, you're just buttering me up," he gulped. "I'll bet you say that to all the guys."

"Just the really handsome ones with busted knees," she answered, moving to sit on the chair's arm. "And it helps if he's really tall and Scottish. Not to mention being a former Marine."

"You left out the Brotherhood Protector part," he said.

"I'm working on it," she promised. "Does your knee feel well enough for us to walk over to the desk and look at the files Sergeant Miller sent? It's only a few steps."

"I might need a wee bit of help," he admitted. "But only a fool would say no to a bonnie lass helping him. And I sure don't want to use that wheelchair."

"My pleasure," she said, getting to her feet so she could help him stand. Putting her arm around his waist, she added, "Sorry about my f'ing language."

"Marines have heard worse, my jungle cat," he

laughed as they hobbled to the desk. "Do you think you could make us a pot of tea before we start? And put just a *wee* bit of whiskey in it? Not even a dram? The bottle is on the bar in the living room."

"I already made it," she announced proudly, easing him into one of the chairs and fetching the hassock. "Except for the whiskey. Should be well brewed by now. I'll be right back."

She returned with a tray and set things out on the desk as Mac switched on the computer and pulled up the file for them to stare at the names and photos of the six missing teenagers.

"So, tell me again what do all these kids have in common?" Mac grimaced as he re-adjusted his leg. "Would you pour some milk in my cup, please? Milk first, then tea."

"They're all good students from six different area high schools who have no major problems with their parents or in their communities," Anne said, handing him the cup. "From left to right, you're looking at Silas Horton, Marie Wallis, Peter Martinez, Gail Madison, Eric Chan, and Katie Johnson, the winners of *Excelsior's* writing contest for high school juniors. I'd only met the others once after we announced the winners in late September. That photo array is the order in which they were abducted but I double-checked my files this morning for their names before we left for Third Friday–"

"Damn." Mac leaned back and adjusted his leg again. "Is it still Friday?"

"It is," Anne said. "What's that old saying? Time flies when you're having fun. Anyway, we have high standards for the winners' maturity level as well as their writing skills. We want them to take it seriously and not have to worry about their behavior. These kids hit all the marks. Other than the usual growing up challenges, they all have tight relationships with their families and no acting out." Thinking of Katie and the lively antics she shared with her younger brothers, she swallowed the lump rising in her throat.

"Unlike some people, I know." Mac's free hand covered one of hers. "None of them rebelled?"

Anne laughed. "Well, Katie got into trouble last year when she led a school-wide old-fashioned sit-in when someone decided to take away the salad bar. Half the student body joined her because they all liked her. And like Katie, they're vegetarians."

Mac's deep, slow laugh soothed her worries for Katie and her friends a bit. "What happened to her?" he asked, picking up a pencil.

"She did three days at the alternative school where she spent her time drafting a proposal advocating for putting vegetarian choices on the schools' menus based on health, supporting local farmers, and benefitting the planet. Her parents backed her all the way. She's a determined one, my Katie."

"Like her aunt," he said. "And I'll bet just as feisty."

Warmth radiated over Anne's face at his praise, but she shrugged. "Yeah, maybe. You'll like her."

I'm looking forward to meeting her when this is all over." Mac pulled over a sheet that Griff had printed for them. "Three boys, three girls, all sixteen years old. Might that be significant as far as The Cadre is concerned?"

"I don't know," Anne admitted. "When I did that article about missing kids in Gainesville, Florida, they were all ages. But as Hank said, demographics for pedophiles change all the time."

"Okay," Mac said. He pointed the pencil at the photos and names displayed on the screen. "Silas Horton and Gail Madison are African American, Eric Chan is Asian American, Peter Martinez is Hispanic American and Marie Wallis and Katie Johnson are Caucasian. Sick as it is, no one can accuse The Cadre of being racist."

"I did a story about child sexual abuse when I was an intern at *Excelsior* my first summer in college," Anne said. "Pedophiles come from all races, ethnicities, and economic classes. Many of them target people they already know and have easy access to, so the kids aren't afraid of them. People like teachers, pastors, and coaches."

"And family." The pencil snapped between Mac's fingers.

Anne nodded. "Yeah, and family. When it's family, it cuts down on the time it takes to gain their trust and groom them. They've got more than enough accessibility." The idea of that made her stomach roll and she quickly sipped her tea.

"I'd like to beat the shit out of every single one of the perverts who would do that to a child." A bright anger simmered in Mac's eyes. "As slowly and as painfully as I could manage."

"Oh, my sweet Lord," Anne stared at the photo array again and put down her cup so quickly that some of the contents danced over its edge and onto the saucer. "That's it. It must be. The photos."

"What? Mac demanded, sitting forward.

"Look at them!" Anne demanded. "What's special about them?"

"Well, they looked posed." Mac squinted at the screen. "Those backdrops would certainly suggest that and-son-of-a-biscuit eater. It's their school photos."

"Someone gave The Cadre copies of these photos," Anne said, excitement lending a tremor to her voice. "And those are from this school year. I know because Katie gave me a copy of hers. Remember what Barclee told us? The Cadre wants 'pretty kids.' Every one of the kids is more than just attractive. They were specifically targeted by The

Cadre for their looks if they're the ones who took them."

"I think it's a near damn certainty that's what happened," Mac said. "Okay, they're good students, really good-looking and budding journalists. Are any of the kids from wealthy families?"

"Not that I recall," Anne said. "They have comfortable lives but are far from wealthy. And remember, Katie's parents told us they hadn't received any kind of ransom demands when we met with them. They'd have called me if that had changed."

"And Miller would have told us if any of the other families received ransom demands," Mac agreed. "From what I remember reading about them, a ransom is not The Cadre's MO. Whichever it is, it still sucks. And Cassie told us The Cadre was going to sell the kids once they got to Atlanta."

Anne choked back the nausea rising in her throat. "Like she said, 'it's sick.'" She edged the paper from under Mac's hand and studied it again. "What are we missing?" she murmured. "What are we–Wait. School buses. They all rode school buses! Where's that report Sergeant Miller sent us with the police interviews with the bus drivers?"

Mac grabbed the pile of printed papers and spread them out over the desk while Anne wisely moved the cups.

"Interviews with all six bus drivers for the six

missing students from six different schools," he announced, holding up a sheet. Reading over it, he said, "All claim they let the kids out in the usual place in their neighborhoods so they could walk home as was their habit. They didn't see anything suspicious or out-of-ordinary. And they were the last kids to be dropped off."

"But what if the drivers–all of them–lied and took them somewhere else?" Anne got up to pace the room. "And what do we know about the drivers' backgrounds? They need references and–"

A new idea began to take shape in her mind, horrific and mind-blowing. "Oh, my Lord," she gasped, returning to sit beside Mac. "It's a conspiracy. It's got to be. The bus drivers, the school photographers–they're all working for The Cadre."

"Would all the schools have used the same photography studio?" Mac asked. "The schools in my hometown did and the studio employed extra people, at least for taking school pictures."

"I don't know," Anne sighed, rubbing her temples. "But Katie's mother will know. She volunteers at Katie's school. It's late, but I could call her."

"I have a better idea." Mac reached into the pocket of his sweatpants and pulled out his phone. After tapping the screen and turning on the speaker, he said, "Hey, Griff. Feel up to a little creative hacking tonight?"

You know how I love pushing the envelope.

What d'ya have in mind?" Griff's confident laugh brought them a welcome sense of relief, and Anne and Mac traded smiles.

"Take that information you've got on the bus drivers and photographers for our six missing kids and scour their backgrounds," Mac directed. "Everything and anything you can find and go really, really deep."

"I'm sensing a conspiracy here," Griff said, using Anne's words and the light-hearted tone vanished from his voice. "Lots of what's been hidden is going to be hauled into the light and we all know what happens then. What do you want me to do about the ledger? I'm making progress but it's a tough nut to crack."

"Can it wait?" Anne implored. "I know it's important, but if we can find something hinky about the drivers and photographers, it might lead us to The Cadre as much as the ledger might."

"Hinky?" Griff asked. "What's that?"

"Hinky," she repeated firmly. "Meaning weird, creepy, and downright horrible. Not to mention smelling really bad."

"Reporters," Mac sighed. "Don't you just love their command of the English language?"

"Gotta love 'em," Griff laughed. "I'll get started on it right now and let you know when I find something." Anne noted he said "when" and not "if."

"We know you will," Mac said. "I'm going to follow Jones' orders and go to bed. It's late."

"You need to rest," Griff agreed. "Catch up with you in the morning. 'Night, Anne."

"Good night, Griff," she said. "And thanks. I owe you one."

"You don't owe me anything," and the ferocity in his voice was a welcome sound. "I'm honored to be a part of the team that's going to find and bring down those scumbags."

"Thanks, buddy." Mac ended the call, sat back, and wiggled his eyebrows at Anne. "Hinky?"

"Katie's brothers use that word all the time," Anne said. "Can Griff really hack into the schools' databases and not get caught?"

Mac laughed. "Oh, yeah. He holds a double major in IT and mathematics from UT Knoxville. Top of his class, wildly creative, and one of BP's top code breakers. He is, as my youngest sister likes to say, 'scary smart.'"

"I'm impressed," Anne said. "And I agree you should follow Dr. Jones' orders and go to bed."

"Do you know?" He leaned in to place a hand on her cheek.

Ignoring the roaring in her ears, Anne nodded. "You know what you said about not being able to put on clean clothing?"

His gentle smile shifted into something totally and temptingly delicious. "Aye. That I do."

"Well," she said, leaning in to brush her lips against his. "I was thinking you might need help taking them off, don't you know. After all, it is bedtime."

"Isn't it just," he whispered, allowing her to help him stand and put her arm around his waist. "Down the hall to the third door on the right," he directed. "That's where I usually sleep."

CHAPTER 14

"Your bed is already turned down," Anne observed. "Is that a BP thing or a Marine thing?"

"It's a MacFarlane thing," he answered. "We like taking naps in the afternoon so we can be rested for the night's activities. You never know what might happen. But I left it that way when I came to the church to meet you just in case you came here. I wanted to make a good impression."

"I like a tidy man," she whispered as they sat on the bed.

They held each other for a while. "Are we sure it's still Friday?" she asked.

"I think it's a wee bit past," Mac told her. "In Scotland, it's way past midnight and the banshees are sure to be howling."

"Are they?" Her attempt at imitating his accent

made them both laugh. "What do we do about that?"

"Leave them be," he advised. 'Tis never wise to mess with a banshee.'

"So what do we do now?" she asked, putting her hands behind his head.

"Perhaps this."

He moved his hands to untie the ribbon at the end of her braid. Slowly, methodically, gently, he pulled apart the strands, enjoying the feel of her hair over his fingers.

"It's a shame you don't have a brush in here," he said. "Don't women brush their hair a hundred strokes before they go to bed?"

"Remember me telling you at Henry's I was a Girl Scout? I'm always prepared." She pulled the comb/brush from her pocket and handed it to him.

"I like a woman who is always prepared," he praised as he turned her around and then began to work the brush through her hair.

Her contented sigh was almost a purr. "I do feel like a cat," she murmured. "Warm and safe."

"I've got a great fondness for cats," he said, dropping the brush to the floor. "Especially when I'm curled up with one."

She turned to face him, her eyes shining with invitation as he slowly reached for the hem of his T-shirt and pulled it over his head. He sat very still, enjoying the feel of her hands against his skin, breathing in the scent of soap and it was as heady as any perfume he'd ever inhaled.

"Will this be your first time? he asked.

"No," she said. "I'm guessing it's not yours either."

"No," he answered. "But it's been a long time."

"Me too." She smoothed her hands through the copper-hued curls covering his chest, lightly flicking her fingertips over his nipples and a quick gasp escaped him.

"Sensitive there?" she whispered.

"That and other places," he sighed. "As you will soon learn."

The warmth from her sudden, demanding kiss cascaded over him and he returned its ferocity, listening to the moan rising from her throat, sweet as the call of a siren.

"Turnabout is fair play," he said taking off her sweater. "Besides, this is big on you."

"Don't you know that oversized clothing for women is all the rage?" she teased.

"I may have sisters, but there's always something new to learn when it comes to women and their fashion," he mused. "But I think you'll find me an eager and attentive pupil."

"Then let the lessons begin," she whispered as his hands moved to take off her bra. "I'm always eager to improve my education."

They stripped each other of their remaining

clothing and rolled onto the bed, and she kicked the covers aside. Lips met lips while hands made a lazy exploration over bodies, fingertips moving gently across sensitive areas, inch by inch, spot by spot, teasing them into excitement.

While they may have made such journeys before, this was new, uncharted territory and they were exploring it together for the first time. Skin brushed skin and their mouths feasted on spots long untasted. Excitement at the newness of it added to their arousal until their breathing and joined bodies locked in the sweetest rocking motion of union that was as old as time itself, launching them into the lovers' abyss of satisfied completion.

Later as they lay under the sheets, and she was nestled against his shoulder, she asked, "Was there a particular reason you joined Tennessee Task Force? Your other work with BP must surely be as important."

"Yeah," he said after a moment. "Remember you asked me the other night who Lily was? When I was eighteen, my BP buddy Parker Evans' youngest sister Lily, who was four years old, was snatched while we were at a county fair. Someone called Parker's name and when he looked around, Lily dropped his hand. A witness said there was a clown-and I mean some person dressed like one–holding a puppy and beckoning to her. Lily was always dog crazy, so it was the perfect setup. It was crowded that day, and in just a few seconds, Lily and the clown were gone. We think they dashed into a nearby funhouse. You know, the ones that are dark and full of mazes the cars on rails move along. Like Katie and the others, we never had a ransom demand and never heard anything from those who took her. Parker beat himself up over it for years, even though his parents never blamed him for a second."

"Oh my," Anne murmured. "What happened after that? To you and Parker, I mean."

"He became a cop who specialized in getting kids out of abusive and neglectful homes. I became an EMT and a medic, and did a lot of trauma work with kids. I joined the Marines a year before Parker did, but we eventually met up again, and served in Afghanistan."

"It's like you have a calling to help kids," Anne suggested. "That's why the death of the Sayyid children hurt you so badly, 'Big Dude'. They saw you as another brother, someone who loved them and they could trust."

"I guess," and Anne's heart ached for the sadness in his voice.

"You are," she insisted. "I'll bet your nephews and nieces are crazy about you and you would do anything to protect them. You'd do anything to help kids."

"Yeah," he whispered, leaning in to kiss her. "But let's not talk about that now."

The twinkle in his eyes set her heart into a galloping motion. "Are we going to go to sleep?"

"Not just yet, my jungle cat," he whispered again. "Not just yet."

CHAPTER 15

"Is that your phone or mine?" Mac murmured, snuggling deeper under the covers and pulling Anne closer to his chest.

"Mine," she sighed and started to ease away but Mac obviously had other ideas and kept his arms firmly in place.

"Let it go to voice mail," he whispered, brushing his lips first against her eyes and then her lips. "Whoever it is, can wait for another hour or so. We have better things to do."

"Like what?" She hadn't imagined he would look this good first thing in the morning. The rumpled, sleepy bear from yesterday was back.

And what his hands were doing proved he was most definitely not sleepy. "Stop," she murmured.

"Does that tickle?" His grin was just a degree short of naughty.

"If you tickle me, you'll need a cast for your knee," she warned, rolling over to grab her phone on the nightstand. "It's Stanley Harris," she said, scrambling from bed and out of his reach. "Hey, Stanley," she greeted through a yawn as she put him on speaker. "What's up?"

"Sorry to bother you so early on a Saturday, but Robert Carsen just announced on national TV that he's running for governor," the familiar voice of her editor announced. "On all the other stations too."

"Botheration," Anne muttered, tucking the phone under her chin. "On national TV? He's not wasting time." She gestured at Mac and mimed pouring coffee. He nodded, grabbed one of the hotel's bathrobes–they'd stopped making love long enough to shower last night before they fell asleep–from the foot of the bed and quickly left, but not so quickly it didn't give her time to admire his lovely well-toned backside. Taking her robe, she slid her arms into the sleeves and knotted it at the waist.

"What do you mean, he's not wasting time?" Stanley asked.

"We heard him do the same thing yesterday at Third Friday," Anne told him as she headed for the kitchen where Mac was pouring out the coffee. They'd programmed the machine the night before. "I went up there to check on some things. What did he say today?"

"Slammed the local police about not doing

enough to find the missing kids, and talked about all the changes he'd make when he was elected," Stanley growled. "Not if, but when."

"You don't get votes by bad-mouthing the police," Anne said, picking up the cups and following a slightly limping Mac into the office. "What a windbag."

"I could think of other things to call him," Mac said, as she put the cups on a low table before a sofa and they sat. "But there's a lady present."

The door to the suite swung open and a voice called, "Anyone at home? Or up?"

"In the office, Griff," Mac called, looking at Anne. "Now we're in for it," he muttered.

She squinted at him. "Why?"

He rolled his eyes. "Silly," he whispered. "Our bathrobes."

"Oops," she whispered back and giggled. "Better he finds out sooner than later."

Griff strolled in, laptop bag over his shoulder. His gaze roamed over them, taking in their bathrobes, sleep-messy hair, and sheepish expressions. Anne's cheeks burned and she could have sworn there were patches of red on Mac's face.

"Stanley, I need to go, but I want to talk to you later about doing a story on The Cadre," she said, staring at the phone's screen. She didn't dare look at Griff.

"I'm not going to let you make yourself a target,

Anne," Stanley said, and she was glad this wasn't a face-to-face call. She could only imagine his expression if he saw them in their robes. His voice carried warning enough.

"I'll be careful," Anne promised quickly. "Look, another BP member has just arrived, possibly with some new facts. I'll call you." She hit the end call and slid the phone into her robe's pocket. "Hi, Griff," she said as casually as she could.

"So," Griff said, his mouth trembling with barely suppressed laughter. "How's the leg?"

"Fine," they chorused simultaneously.

"Well," he drawled, "I come bearing tidings of great joy. Took most of the night, so I could use some of that coffee."

"You do look tired," Anne said quickly, eager to change his focus. "Let me get you a cup."

"Black, if you don't mind," he called as she hurried to the kitchen but not before she heard Griff's distinct chuckle followed by what sounded like a low-pitched threat. Grabbing a cup from the cupboard, filled it and returned to the office. "Have you found something?" she asked, handing him the cup.

"Have I ever." Accepting the cup, Griff went to sit at the large, kidney-shaped desk with its wide screen and engaged the computer. "I'm still trying to break the ledger. It's starting to make sense, but I spent most of my time hacking into the school system's employment files. First, I checked on the bus drivers since they were the last ones to see the kids. It turns out that other than knowing how to drive school buses, all the references and background information those six men submitted are false, right down to their social security numbers."

"They wanted to hide who they were," Anne guessed. "You have to have nearly perfect references to drive school buses because of the liability."

"I'd say you're right, Anne," Griff agreed. "You could have a driving record that would almost qualify you to drive for NASCAR, but if you're not safe around kids? Forget it."

"So how did these guys pull it off?" Mac asked. "How did they get it past the schools, let alone the bus companies with phony references and social security numbers?"

"Because whoever is behind this put up a dummy website for employers to view." Griff's eyes sparkled in triumph, but his voice was deadly serious. "If I try to get a job driving a school bus, both the bus company and the school could go out to this website and boom! There's all the information they need, including my references, that makes me look like the perfect candidate for the job. I'm hired and have easy access to kids. I'm not sure how they managed to get routes with high school kids but maybe drivers can state what age kids they prefer driving."

"So the website is some kind of cover?" Mac repeated as if he were considering what he'd heard. "And *all* the drivers' identities are false?"

Griff nodded. "Every one of them. The schools would never have known once the website references vetted them."

"I think you're having way too much fun with this," Anne declared. "What else did you find?"

The Marine's expression shifted from satisfaction to one of barely contained rage. "That every one of those drivers is on the national registry for sex offenders. The photographers too."

"But sex offenders can't live anywhere near schools or in neighborhoods with kids under eighteen, much less drive school buses or work with kids!" Mac protested. "Unless you've been living under a rock for the past thirty years, everyone knows that."

"Hence the need for false identities," Anne said softly. "They'd have to have them, otherwise no school system would hire them."

"Imagine the fallout if that website had helped hide pedophiles who are now working as teachers or teachers' aides?" Mac added. "Are the photographers working for the same agency?"

"The local school system has used *Carlyle's*, a local photography company for years," Griff shared. "Talk about a perfect cover. And like *Randolph's*, the bus company, hired a bunch of new staff earlier this year, right about the time we think The Cadre came to town. All of them have lived somewhere in East Tennessee for at least ten years, but by the first of the year they'd all moved to Knoxville."

"Dear Lord," Anne gasped. "We were right. It was–is a conspiracy. I think I'm going to be sick."

"The Cadre hired the photographers to find the 'pretty kids' as Barclee called them, and the bus drivers snatched them," Mac said grimly. "What the hell are these men getting out of this? Money? The kid of their choice?" Rage tightened his features and his hands knotted into fists. "If even one of them has touched those kids, I swear to God I will beat the crap out of them. We need to call Miller right now. Griff, can you forward him what you've found?"

"With pleasure," Griff said, punching the keyboard.

Mac took his phone from the pocket of his robe, tapped the screen, and turned on the speaker. He nodded at Anne and then said, "Sergeant Miller? MacFarlane here. Don't ask me how we know, but the bus drivers for those six kids and the school photographers? They're all pedophiles."

"Holy Mother of God," Miller sputtered. "Are you sure?"

"We're forwarding the information even as we speak," Mac assured him. "Just don't ask how–"

"I don't give a damn how you learned it or found it," Miller interrupted. "I'll let the lawyers deal with that. But for now, I'm sending out the black and whites to haul their asses down to the station. Praise the Lord it's Saturday and the drivers aren't driving. Do you have the photographers' addresses?"

"Sent it to you with the other stuff," Griff confirmed.

"Thank you," Miller said. "By day's end, we'll have at least one of them talking."

"Oh, one more thing. Cassie Douglas left despite Lt. Tyler finding her a place to stay. She said her old man would beat her ass if she didn't show up with her earnings. And we had a whole bunch of drunks brought in about that time so she left. Sorry."

"That's too bad," Anne sighed. "I was hoping we could help her."

"Nothing to be done," Max said. "Let us know what you find."

"Will do," Miller said as Anne's phone buzzed with a text message. Glancing at the screen, she said, "It's Katie's mother. "She wants to know if I saw Carsen's speech this morning. She's upset about him saying the police aren't doing anything to find the kids."

"Based on what Harris told us, I can't blame

her," Mac said. "The TV is set to tape all the news channels, so we'll have to watch it later."

"I'm going to call her and suggest the families get together later today so we can tell them that we think we have a break," Anne said. "Just enough to give them some hope and to tell them to ignore what Carsen said."

"I'll text Miller to tell him of that plan," Mac called as she hurried from the room, and he permitted himself to put the situation at hand on the back burner for just a few seconds to watch the elegant sway of her hips as she walked.

"Feeling better, are we?" Griff chuckled softly. "Got enough rest last night, did we?"

"Shut up, Griff," Mac said pleasantly. "Shouldn't you go back to trying to break the ledger's code?"

Griff's serious mood returned. "I have a date later this morning to visit some pedophile chat rooms out on the Dark Web to see what they know about kids being easily available in this area. Maybe some of 'our guys'–if you'll pardon the expression–will be there."

"You've done that before?" Mac stared at his colleague. He hadn't known Griff very long and didn't know what he did before joining Brotherhood Protectors, but he had a feeling the man had more than a little experience in subterfuge.

"Oh yes," Griff drawled, a dangerous glitter entering his eyes. "I've several identities for visiting such places and more than once some monster has walked right into the trap and found themselves facing a very long prison sentence. Trust me, those suckers will never know who Loves Little Boys–that's my handle–is. Just wish I could be at one of the bus driver's homes when Miller's boys show up in their driveways, blue lights flashing. We're so close to finding out who's behind this and finding the kids, I can smell it."

"I'm damn glad to have you on my team, Griff," Mac told him. "Your computer and hacking expertise are more than welcome."

"I've got nephews and nieces," Griff told him. "And if we ever got a chance to beat the shit out of these people, I'll be right there with you. Our boss, however, frowns on such displays of violence." Abruptly he laughed, and added, "But since we're never on screen when these groups meet, I don't have to wear a disguise. Taking off all that make-up is a pain in the ass."

"The parents all want to meet this afternoon at one o'clock," Anne announced, rejoining them. "I suggested we meet in the downstairs conference room, so Mac won't have to travel with his injured leg, and they agreed."

"Griff's going to play on the Dark Web and catch some more bad guys," Mac told her. "Pedophile chatrooms."

Anne settled herself on the sofa again and

fought the urge to lean against him. "You can get into the Dark Web and not be detected? Just how good of a hacker are you?"

"He's a genius," Mac said simply. "Did I forget to mention he has a Master's Degree in IT and Web Design from MIT? He can hack into anything, and no one will ever know he's been there."

"And we're gonna take those suckers down," Griff promised. "I love it when that happens. I'm going to get back to working on the ledger until my meeting starts. Touch base with me after you meet with the parents."

He ambled from the suite and the door clicked closed behind him. When she was sure he was gone, Anne looked at the man beside her. "Since it's only nine o'clock, what's the best use of our time?" she asked.

"Well." Mac sounded thoughtful. "My leg still feels a wee bit swollen. I was thinking maybe having a bit of a lie-down for an hour or so might be helpful."

Her heart took off at a mad gallop, Anne said, "The doctor did say you should stay off of it for a while," and desire heated her face. "And since you didn't get a lot of sleep last night–"

"And who's fault might that be?" Mac's lips started exploring her hair, her eyes, and her neck and she purred in contentment.

"–don't interrupt," Anne gasped. "Maybe a short

nap would help. In your leg's recovery, that is."

"I think that's a fine idea," and the now beloved accent crept into his voice. "And I was also thinking, don't you know, that I might need someone nearby just in case I needed something. A glass of water or a cup of tea or something like that."

"I could do that," Anne offered, palming his face. "When I was a kid, I thought briefly about being a doctor, so I practiced on my sisters' dolls. They said I had a wonderful bedside manner."

"I'd have to see that before I believe it," he whispered, pulling them to their feet. "We Scots are suspicious and take a lot of convincing. Demonstrations are helpful, don't you know."

He moved as if to lift her into his arms, but she pulled back. "Don't even think about picking me up, 'Scotty'", she warned. "I'll bet I could carry you if needed."

"Big talk from such a wee slip of a lass," he teased but his desire turned his eyes to a golden bronze. "But would you be lettin' me put my arm around your waist, so I don't fall over when we walk back to bed?"

"I think I can do that," she whispered, accepting his touch and slowly walking them to the bedroom.

And there, in the unmade bed, they took their time, discovering new pleasures and revisiting old ones until taking a nap became necessary, and they slept the sleep of those who love.

CHAPTER 16

LATER SATURDAY MORNING.

"YOU'RE SURE the girl will arrive tonight, tomorrow at the latest? The investors are getting impatient for the delivery of the others. They do not like being disappointed or made to wait too long. There might be–consequences." The deep, raspy voice with its veiled threat was more than malicious. It was evil. Pure evil and sweat broke out on Hobert Scaren's forehead.

Scaren did not scare easily. He was too careful, too methodical in laying his plans. Every detail needed to be spelled and carried out to perfection. One does not rise to the top by being careless or relying on those who prove to be incapable or disloyal. Otherwise, one can fail. Scaren did not like a failure. He had not built his empire of success on failure.

But this person, his contact, from The Cadre "creeped him out" as his grandchildren would say. The person behind the desk in their secret meeting place, as usual, wore a low-brimmed hat and sunglasses. Except for a sliver of light from a tiny window high in a corner of a wall, the room was in near darkness and Scaren was grateful. Sitting with his knees against the metal desk, he did not need his contact to see how frightened he was.

"The girl was ill with her–" Scaren hesitated over which word to use. His contact was already annoyed with him and Scaren knew just what The Cadre could do when displeased. He had no wish to offend their emissary. "Her monthly flow," he finally said.

"This situation is now under control?" The voice rose ever-so-slightly.

"As of yesterday," Scaren assured.

"Be sure she is clean for twenty-four hours. Her buyer does not like soiled goods. When she is clean twenty-four hours, bring her to Knoxville. The final transport must begin tomorrow evening at the latest."

"Absolutely." Scaren hesitated again, then asked. "When will I receive the rest of the payment?"

"When the goods are delivered, and the customers are satisfied," the voice rasped.

Scaren dared to laugh. "You saw the photos of all of them," he chortled. "How could anyone not be satisfied? You asked for beauty and that's what you're getting."

A flick of his contact's hand brought forward the man standing near the door in a burst of speed and strength. His hands around Scaren's neck were smooth, almost soft, but like iron in their grip, tightening ever so slowly until Scaren was gasping for air.

"It is unwise to argue or offend The Cadre," his contact's voice purred. "We are called Los Silenciosos–Silent Ones–for a reason. And though almost none of us can claim any Spanish heritage, the name is most effective in instilling terror, is it not? Do you know why people have such fear for us? Because no one ever sees us coming until it's too late. Release him."

The hands moved from Scaren's neck only to grab and slam his head against the metal desk and hold it there. The cold surface against Scaren's cheek was like ice and he groaned as fingers tightened around his neck again.

"Do not underestimate us again," his contact warned. "The consequences could be–unpleasant."

The hands moved and gasping, Scaren sat up and rubbed his throat. "I understand," he croaked.

"Very good," his contact praised. "One small detail remains. Find Anne Hamilton and kill her.

She has created too many problems for our clients. I want to see the body."

Satisfaction at the command nearly erased Scaren's fear. "I can do that," he said smugly.

"You have failed to do so three times before." The evil note returned to his contact's voice. "Do so again, and we will find someone else to complete our mission. At the cost of your life. Go."

The hands grabbed Scaren again and dragged him to the door. A masked figure he had not seen opened it and he found himself shoved into an alley. In the distance, he could hear the roar of traffic from Neyland Drive and the fainter sound of music from Neyland Stadium. He'd forgotten about the football game today. Fear for your life can do that to a man.

He leaned against the alley wall, mopping his face with the initialed handkerchief he always carried, and waited for his ragged breathing to slow. The only thing keeping him from collapsing in a heap was the order to find Anne Hamilton and kill her. The little bitch was more trouble than she was worth and Scaren would take great pleasure in how he would kill her.

The challenge would be how to get her away from that Marine turned Brotherhood Protector. At least the guy he sent after them last night had disabled MacFarlane, slowing him down. Or so he said. Scaren needed to be sure someone at the jail silenced him before he could start squawking.

But he hadn't killed them. No matter. Scaren would now have that pleasure. And he would be damn sure MacFarlane was watching when Anne Hamilton died.

Then hoping he'd brought enough cash to tip the driver well, he all but ran to where the taxicab waited.

Early Saturday afternoon

"We've busted four of the bus drivers and six of the photographers," Miller reported with a grin as they stood outside the conference room at *Ramsey's.* "The first thing we did was confiscate their phones. I'll be blessed if their one call will be to tip off the others."

"Do you think they'll have hidden stuff on them?" Mac asked. Spending the morning making love to Anne had left him, except for his knee, feeling calm and relaxed.

We've already got our techs taking the phones apart to see what might be hidden," Miller said, his grin widening. "We're out looking for the others now. And with a little help from our friends at DVM, we have the makes of the others' cars and license plates. It's just a matter of time before we have them all."

"That's great news!" Anne exclaimed and Mac fought the urge to put his arms around her. He could only guess what a toll this was taking on her. Between bouts of lovemaking, she'd told him funny stories about Katie, and it was obvious she loved the girl like her own. He'd shared more of his memories of Lily Evans and those of some of the kids he'd known during his work as an EMT.

Now, it looked like they were closing in on The Cadre, and he wondered what would happen between them when it was over. Best not to think about that now. "Anything else you can tell us, Sergeant Miller?" Mac asked now.

"Yeah. Your attacker is a guy named Alan Petti-grew," Miller reported. "Thirty-six years old with a rap sheet as long as your arm with charges all over the Midwest. He's mostly an enforcer, who intimi-dates or beats up people. The funny thing is, he's a local who's only recently returned to East Tennessee. He's one nasty customer. Of course, with his nose and cheekbones broken, thanks to Anne, he's not doing much talking except to say he's going to sue her."

"I'm not worried about that," Anne declared. "I'll just claim it was self-defense. Do you think you can share some of what's happened with the parents?" Her excitement lit up her face, giving her skin a luminous glow. "We're getting so close, I want them to have more hope than they've had for the past three weeks."

"I can give them an edited version," Miller agreed. "When I left, most of those guys were still yelling about lawyers and suing us, but like you, Anne, we're not worried about that."

"Let's meet the parents," Mac suggested. "I hate to sound like a wimp, but my knee is starting to bother me."

He let Anne open the door and led them into the meeting room. Six couples, all wearing name tags, were clustered around a table. As they entered, their gazes all went straight to Anne, calling out to her in greeting, and Mac remembered her describing meeting them at a celebration for their kids winning *Excelsior's* writing contest.

But just as quickly, their gazes took in Miller, and the tenor of the room shifted. Questions were shouted and several of the fathers rose, but Anne quickly took charge, her soothing voice calming them a bit, and they sat again, waiting. Mac chose a chair in the corner of the room and sat back, watching.

"I believe you all know Sergeant Miller, who has been one of the leads in this case," she said with a gentle authority. "I hope you'll agree what he has to share with you is good news. Sergeant Miller?" She smiled at him and joined Mac in the corner.

Miller stepped forward and Mac admired his calm. Facing parents of abducted kids must feel like Daniel walking into the lions' den. But the police officer's expression was professional and courteous, and he got straight to the point.

"This morning, we've had a major break in the case." He had to wait for the gasps and cheers to die down before he could continue. "After unearthing some information, we're holding a few 'people of interest' for questioning. There is also good reason to believe that more than one of them knows something about where your sons and daughters are."

"Do you know where they are?" shouted Teresa Wallis.

"Do you even know if they're alright?" Fredrick Madison's question was also a shout.

"We don't know where they are," Miller admitted, "but we have no reason to believe that they've come to any kind of harm and that they are most likely being held close by."

"Yeah, well, Robert Carsen thinks the police aren't doing enough," accused Roger Horton. "What do you have to say about that?"

"Yeah, three weeks and no leads?" Tobias Wallis chimed in. "What do you say about that?"

For the first time since he'd met Miller, Mac watched the officer's face redden and the atmosphere in the room vibrated with unspoken fear and anger.

"Mr. Carsen," Miller began, but Mac rose and came to stand beside him. Miller was above average height, but Mac towered over him.

"Excuse me, Sergent Miller, may I? I'd like to say something to these good people." Offering up the Gaelic prayer warriors used before battle, Mac began.

"Ladies and gentlemen, my name is Lt. Keith MacFarlane, USMC retired. I met Sergeant Miller last spring when he and I became a part of the Tennessee Task Force, a new, multi-agency organization dedicated to finding and rescuing missing children. Our first case, which ended successfully I might add, was only done because of men like Sergeant Miller, who are working round the clock to find your children."

He had their full attention and Mac gathered his compassion for these families whose lives had been made a living hell because of The Cadre. And they couldn't even tell them that they knew The Cadre had their children.

"I can't imagine the nightmare, the sheer hell of what you've experienced these past few weeks," he continued. "I have nephews and nieces and if something like this happened to them, I'd be tearing out my beard from worry."

"It's a nice beard," Clarie Johnson said shyly, and

the other women laughed while the men seemed to relax.

Mac grinned, allowing just a trace of his accent to enter his voice. "I'm told if a fellow keeps it trimmed, it doesn't tickle the ladies too much when you kiss them. But because of my past work with KPD, I can tell you, they're doing everything humanly possible to find your kids and arrest the monsters that took them. Forget what Carsen is saying and trust Miller and his men. They're going to find your children and bring them home, safe and sound."

He returned to his place in the corner and the tension in the room lessened as the parents nodded and whispered among themselves. Only one, Marcia Chan remained belligerent.

"What if those people you're talking to ask for attorneys?" she demanded. "You know, 'lawyer up'?"

"That's their right," Miller reminded them. "We can't stop them from doing that." Then he smiled and Mac had to hold back his laughter as Miller added, "But based on the information we have, they're going to need lawyers. Very good lawyers."

"We're going to let you continue talking with Sergeant Miller as long as you want or need," Anne said. "Thank you for coming today."

"Are you going to write about all this when we're done, Ms. Hamilton?" called Oscar Martinez.

It was her turn to grin and Mac's heart turned over at the triumph sparkling in her eyes. "With the biggest font *Excelsior* has!" she shouted, and the parents cheered.

She gestured for him to follow her, and they slipped into the lobby, closing the door behind them. Her beautiful, brilliant smile was the final blow and Mac surrendered his heart. He just hoped, prayed there was a chance she felt the same way.

"You were magnificent in there," she praised.

He shrugged. "Can't have them dumping on Miller. The man's worked his ass off. What do we do now?"

"If your knee is up for driving, I thought we'd take a little trip across town."

"Did ye?" Slipping into Scottish mode always made him more confident, especially around women. "Where to?"

"The Bartlett-Sims Animal Shelter about doing a story on volunteers."

CHAPTER 17

A SHORT WHILE later

"It occurred to me I'd never gone to the animal shelter to ask them about our kids all doing volunteer work there," Anne said as they drove west. "I haven't had time, and I didn't want to get in the way of the police investigation. But maybe we could learn something if we offer to do a story about them."

"Free publicity couldn't hurt," Mac agreed. "What else will you tell them?"

Anne thought a moment. "In addition to asking them about their history and their recent remodel, I'll tell them I want to do a story about volunteer opportunities at the shelter, especially for teens. That will be an easy way to ask about the kids without making them suspicious. And of course, why adopting from a shelter is such a good idea."

"Sounds good to me." Mac wiggled his eyebrows at her. "Who am I supposed to be?"

Anne dug in her purse, pulled out a camera on a strap, and hung it around his neck. Just touching his shoulders sent her pulse up several notches. "My photographer," she said.

"Are you always so prepared?" he teased.

"Like I said, I was Girl Scout," she boasted. "Wanna hear about all my merit badges?"

"Maybe some other time," he said, as they pulled into the shelter's spacious parking lot. "But I'll bet there are a bunch of them."

The shelter neighborhood was not far from the university district but gave the feel of being in open country, with several old and boarded-up buildings, including what looked to be an old silo with a high observation deck.

"That's an old bread factory," Anne told him as they got out of the truck. "The original owner was a bit eccentric and liked to stand up there and look out over Knoxville. Of course, that was a hundred years ago, and he could see the mountains more clearly then."

"Maybe when this is over, we could take a trip up to the mountains," Mac said as they walked to the front door. "I enjoyed our trip to Peaksville."

Excitement pulsed through Anne again at the

thought of sharing the beauty of her state with him, but she simply said, "That sounds like fun."

Inside, the lobby was bright and colorful. On either side were large rooms, one with oversized cages for the dogs and the other with climbing "trees" for the cats. A young woman wearing an orange and white University of Tennessee sweatshirt looked up from behind a desk and smiled. "Good afternoon! I'm Nancy. Welcome to the Bartlett-Sims Animal Shelter. How may I help you?"

"I'm Anne Hamilton from *Excelsior*," she said. "This is my photographer, Keith MacFarlane." Saying his given name sounded strange, almost as if naming someone she'd never met. "I'd like to speak to someone about doing a story on the shelter."

"You're in luck," Nancy said. "Barry Phillips, our director is here today." She pointed at a man in the cat room and waved to get his attention. "We're getting ready to do a transport of dogs to Michigan tomorrow."

"Michigan?" Mac asked and Anne swallowed a laugh as he peered through the camera's lens, moving the camera around as if deciding what to photograph first.

Nancy nodded. "Oh, yeah. There's a shortage of adoptable dogs in some northern cities. Hey, Barry–" she waved at the man from the cat room as he entered the lobby. "These folks want to do a story about the shelter."

"Glad to hear it!" Like Nancy, Barry Phillips wore a UT sweatshirt. "We go causal on game day," he said with a laugh, plucking at the sweatshirt. "Let me show you around."

He led them through the well-lit, cheerful facility, Mac snapping pictures as they went from room to room.

They ended up in Phillips' office and for a moment, Anne froze. Behind his desk was a blown-up photograph of a group of smiling people, some holding cats, one with a bird on their shoulder, and others holding leashes attached to a group of very happy-looking dogs. In the front row, were all six of the missing kids.

And unless she was very mistaken, the woman standing behind Katie Johnson, hands on her shoulders, was Cassie Douglas. Beside her, she felt Mac stiffen and heard him quietly take in and release a long breath.

"Something wrong?" Phillips asked as he gestured at the chairs in front of his desk.

"No," Anne said quickly as they sat. Taking her writing pad and pen from her purse, she added, "Just amazed by the volume of your work."

They sat, and Phillips shared the history of the shelter, its no-kill mission, and dedication to finding every animal if not a forever home, then at least a good foster one. Anne nodded but kept her gaze on her pad as she took notes, surprised the pen didn't slip from her trembling fingers. Looking up, she gave Phillips her most professional smile. "Nancy out front mentioned something about the shelter sometimes finding homes for dogs in other states. Is that right?"

"It is," Phillips affirmed. "We have a van taking a group of dogs to the Detroit area tomorrow." He laughed and added, "We've found that on a game weekend, there's less traffic early on Sunday morning 'cause folks sleep late. Especially when UT wins!"

"Do you allow teenagers to be volunteers?" Anne asked, pointing at the photo. "Seems like it would be a good community service project."

Phillips' laughter stopped and he sighed. "We do," he said sadly. "As a reporter, I'm sure you've heard about those six kids that disappeared. All of them were–are–volunteers here. Started here last spring, and not a nicer bunch of kids you'd ever find. It's just sickening to think something bad has happened to them."

He swiveled in his office chair and pointed at the photo. "That's from the day after we finished our remodel," he explained. "And that's the kids in the front row."

Anne nodded and was struck again by just how amazingly attractive the six kids were. She squinted at the photo and asked, "Would you have a copy of that by any chance?"

"I do." Phillips opened a drawer in his desk and pulled out a photo. "Are you going to do a story about the kids?"

"I'm not sure," Anne hedged as Mac took the offered photo. "I'd need to check with the police. I don't want to upset their parents. They've been through enough already."

"Who's that?" Mac pointed at the woman standing behind Katie. "She looks familiar."

"That's Issac E. Galouds," Philips said. "But we call her Izzy. She started volunteering here this past spring too. She's our Scottish volunteer."

"She's from Scotland?" Mac asked. "Really? Is she a good volunteer? Good with the kids?"

"She's a trooper," Phillips said, some of his enthusiasm returning. "We've never had a volunteer from Scotland before. We're all crazy about her accent."

Scottish my ass. If that's not Cassie Douglas, I'll trade in my kilt. "I'll bet you are," Mac said softly. "I have lots of Scottish friends, but I've never heard of a name like that or seen it spelled that way."

"It is a funny spelling," Phillips agreed. "She said the grandfather who raised her was a preacher whose favorite Bible story was about Issac and that's how he spelled it."

"Do you suppose she'd let me interview her?"

Anne asked, and Mac watched her making some more notes. "Maybe we could compare and contrast animal shelters here and in Scotland."

"I don't know. She's awfully shy, only comes in a couple of times a month," Phillips said. "She told Nancy that her boyfriend is very jealous and doesn't like her to have any friends, so she can only come in when he goes out of town. But–" His face brightened. "She's coming in tomorrow to assist with the animal transport to Michigan. Maybe you could come by and schedule an interview for when she returns."

"Thanks," Anne said, and Mac heard the barely contained excitement in her voice. "We'll do that. Would you write down her name for me, please? It's so unusual I don't want to forget it."

"Certainly." Phillip scrawled across a sticky note and handed her the sheet. "There you go."

They thanked him and exited the building. Stopping by a large potted rosemary bush, Mac looked at his companion. "Are you thinking what I'm thinking? Except for that name, I'd swear in open court the woman in that group photo is Cassie Douglas."

"It is," Anne said. "Issac E. Galouds is an anagram for Cassie Douglas." Look." She held out her pad. In her neat writing, she'd written Issac E. Galouds, and underneath, Cassie Douglas.

"Damn, you're good," Mac praised. "Where did you learn to do that?"

"I grew up doing crossword and acrostic puzzles they had in the newspaper," she said. "Remember me saying Henry and I used to have contests? And I routinely win at Scrabble at my library branch."

"Why am I not surprised?" Mac chuckled. "But why would Cassie change her name? And why something so outlandish?"

"Maybe because she's ashamed of being a prostitute?" Anne suggested, but she sounded doubtful. "If they did a background check and found she'd been arrested for solicitation, they might not want her working with the public or around kids."

"Somehow I don't think so," Mac said. Let's call Miller before we go back to *Ramsey's.*"

They waved at some of the volunteers who were exercising dogs in large fenced-in areas off from the parking lot and Anne said, "I think you're probably right. Cassie is probably–"

The crackle of a gunshot and an exploding planter sent them diving behind an SUV. Screams came from inside the enclosure, followed by the yelps and howls of terrified dogs.

"Get inside! Now!" Mac roared. The panicked volunteers didn't need to be told twice and they made a mad dash back into the building. Snatching his service revolver from inside his jacket, Mac got into a crouching position and inched to peer around the SUV. "Don't move," he hissed.

"I'm staying right here," Anne said, grabbing her phone from her purse and punching the surface. "Where are the shots coming from?"

"From that silo," Mac snarled, rage pounding through his body.

The splintering glass hit the ground nearby as another shot shattered the windshield of Mac's truck. He released a volley of curses, not caring who heard him. In the distance, the all too familiar wail of a police siren pierced the air.

"That will be Miller." Anne moved to crouch beside him. "Are you alright?"

"Remember what you said about BP's expense account paying for having your clothing dry-cleaned?" Mac kept his gaze locked on the silo. "Well, my truck's windshield just got added to it."

CHAPTER 18

"Do you think Sergeant Miller is getting tired of seeing us so often?" Anne joked. "I don't think a day has gone by since this began that we've not met or at least talked."

"Heaven forbid we should leave him out of all the fun we're having," Mac responded. "It wouldn't be polite."

They'd finally made it back to *Ramsey's* after filing yet another police report about the attack at the animal shelter, including what they'd learned and suspected about Cassie Douglas. An abandoned high-powered rifle was found at the silo's observation deck with several spent casings, but nothing else. Miller promised to get Mac's truck cleared as evidence in another crime scene as soon as possible and have his men out looking for Cassie.

Now after dinner from the hotel's dining room and sending Hank Patterson Anne's theory about Cassie's name being an anagram, Anne, Mac, and Griff sat around the large table in the suite's tech room facing Hank's image on the wide monitor. Hank had called Abel Jones to examine Mac and Anne to be sure their injuries were limited to scrapes from hitting the pavement and Mac's knee was no worse for wear.

"I'm not sure if going to the animal shelter was such a good idea," Hank sighed. "They're following you."

"But now we have good reason to think that Cassie Douglas is involved," Anne insisted. She pointed at the shelter's photo they had blown up and taped to the wipe board propped on an easel. "That's the woman we met who calls herself Cassie Douglas. OK, maybe she's the stereotypical hooker with a heart of gold, but I don't believe that. And I don't believe in coincidences. If Issac E. Galouds and Cassie Douglas were the same person, she would have met all the missing kids."

"That was damn clever figuring about the names," Griff said.

"And now we're thinking she's part of The Cadre," Mac added. "What better cover than posing as a prostitute? Miller told us they've only been aware of her since the first of the year, but we've no idea how long she's been here under another identity."

"I need to brief you on a developing situation there in Knoxville that may have a connection with all of this," Hank said. "We have an operative who's infiltrated a new right-wing militia-style group called Sons of the Smoky Mountains."

"It's not you, is it, Griff?" Anne teased. "With your talent for disguise, you could slip in anywhere."

"Not this time," Griff returned. "I'm having too much fun hanging out with you guys."

"Our operative has learned," Hank continued with a smile, "that there's a huge shipment of guns coming into Knoxville from the Midwest any day now, probably out of Chicago."

"Home of The Cadre." Mac grimaced as he re-adjusted his leg on the hassock. "What do Sons of the Smoky Mountains have to do with this case?"

"And what do we know about them?" Anne asked, taking her writing pad and pen from her nearby purse and Mac wondered if she was ever without them.

"The Sons' mission is to one day launch a

violent take-over of America," Hank described. "The founder's name is Hobert Scaren. He stays in the shadows, so no one in the local chapter– including our plant–has seen or met him. But he reportedly has very deep pockets to finance their operations. We've also learned he was the silent partner for a similar group named Bad Ass Boys, in that area seven years ago, but it died out before anything happened. But we think he–"

"Wait." Anne leaned forward. "Did you say Bad Ass Boys?"

"Do you know about them?" Hank's eyebrows rose.

"As a matter of fact, yes," Anne said. "They were a loosely knit organization of homegrown want-a-be's here in East Tennessee with a vision for a new conservative America. They claimed to be super tough, but they could never get their act together. They dissolved seven years ago."

"Right after you wrote that story about them and made them look like idiots," Mac recalled with a laugh. "They packed their tents and slunk away into the night."

"That was them," Anne said. "I don't remember them as being violent, but then they weren't around very long."

"I don't know if it's the same group newly formed, but they're nothing to be laughed at now," Hank warned. "Our plant says they're buying up guns like crazy, probably from The Cadre but other sources as well. Griff, you've been working on this all afternoon. Have your genius hacking skills found anything about Scaren?"

"Not yet," Griff says regretfully. If he's buried, he's buried as deep as our plant."

"Oh, my Lord," Anne gasped, holding up her pad. "No. It can't be."

The men exchanged glances and then looked at her. "What is it, Anne?" Hank asked.

"Hobert Scaren. It's another anagram. Like Issac E. Galouds is for Cassie Douglas." She went to the whiteboard, took up a marker, and printed the man's name. "Take a look at it," she said. "Mac, think about who else we've seen over the past few days who might have a similar agenda."

His brows drew together as he squinted at the board. Then his eyes widened and his mouth fell open. If their situation hadn't been so dire, Anne would have laughed at his expression.

"Robert H. Carsen?" Mac's voice suggested he didn't believe his question. He rose and limped to the whiteboard to take the marker from Anne and printed the name under that of Scaren. "Well, I'll be the Loch Ness Monster," he said. "It's the same."

"Well, I'm not the Loch Ness Monster," Griff said. "Who is Robert H. Carsen?"

"He's a local businessman who is politically conservative and very, very rich," Anne said. "He just announced his candidacy for governor and has been bad-mouthing the police for their handling of this case. With his fortune, he would have more than enough money to buy all the guns he wanted."

"But what if this time, Carsen isn't only buying guns," Mac said softly. "What if it's an exchange? Our missing kids for guns. Sick as it is, it makes sense."

"And that makes Carsen a conspirator with The Cadre in the kid's abduction!" Anne practically shouted. "He's acting as their broker. Remember what Barclee told us? The Cadre buys 'pretty children'. What do you want to bet it was Carsen and not The Cadre who hired the bus drivers and photographers to find and snatch the kids?"

"Whichever way it is, the bastard is gonna go down," Griff said. "No way he can plead his way out of this."

"And what if Cassie–or whatever her name is–was the first one to see the kids at the shelter?" Mac limped back to his chair and put his leg up again. "She could be just as important a player in this as Carsen. Griff, was Carsen's name on any of the pedophile sites?"

"You have to remember everyone at those sites uses a handle, like I do," Griff reminded them. "But thanks to Anne figuring out about the names being anagrams, give me a little time and I'll try scrambling that into other names. If he's there, I'll find him."

"Could you find out if the bus drivers and the photographers were members of Sons of the Smoky Mountains?" Hope surged through Anne. "Of course, as you say, they'd probably use pseudonyms or handles or–"

"You leave that to me," Griff said, and Anne knew he'd caught her excitement. "My brain is already firing away."

He sprang from the room and Anne returned to perch on the arm of Mac's chair. "Wow," she breathed. "Simply wow. What a story this is going to make!"

"Indeed, it is," Hank agreed. "Now, before we're all too excited to sleep, I think we need to call our new BFF, Sergeant Miller, and bring him up to speed on this latest piece of news. If this doesn't get some of the men he arrested today to start talking, short of thumb screws, I don't know what will."

"I hope he finds Cassie before she leaves for Michigan tomorrow," Anne declared. "I have some questions of my own I'd like to ask her."

They laughed, and Anne noticed some of the tension had vanished from Hank's expression. Mac, on the other hand, looked completely worn out. She needed to take him to bed soon.

And then the images *that* suggested heated her

face so quickly that her cheeks burned, and she had no doubt she was blushing.

"Something wrong?" The subject of her thoughts asked.

"No, no," she said hastily. "Just imagining the expression on Carsen's face when Miller talks to him."

"All members!" Griff shouted as he returned to the room. "Every last stinking one of those guys are members of the Sons of the Smoky Mountains. I just forwarded the whole thing to Miller. We've got 'em!"

"Then I'd say we're done for the day," Hank said simply. "Let's let Miller and his men do their work. They'll contact us as needed. A good night's rest is for all of us."

"I just wish I'd been able to crack Henry's codes," Griff said wistfully. "We might be missing a whole lot more stuff."

"You've done more than enough," Anne praised. "We wouldn't have learned those men are pedophiles if it weren't for you."

"Damn straight," Mac said. "Listen to the lady if you know what's good for you."

"Say good night, Griff," Hank ordered from the screen.

"Good night, Griff," BP's computer whiz echoed and with another laugh, Hank signed off.

"I'm still going to have a crack at that ledger."

Griff stood and his expression was so fiercely determined, Anne knew there was no arguing with him. "I'll be in the computer lab down the hall. Get some rest you two. If you can."

He ducked at the pillow Mac chucked at him and laughing, left them alone.

"And so here we are," Anne sighed. "We're almost done. Let's pray that this time tomorrow the kids will be home safe and sound and sleeping in their own beds."

"Amen," Mac said quietly. "I just hope that after all this, they'll be able to sleep."

Her own sense of exhaustion and living on nerves for nearly seven days swept over Anne. "We never could have done this without Brotherhood Protectors," she whispered. "Without you. I am so sorry I was such a bitch the first day we met."

"I believe," the BP member said, returning her whisper, "that apology has already been made and accepted. I think what we both need right now is to do as Hank suggests and get some rest."

The ferocious beat of Anne's heart banged with a rib-bruising force, and she slowly inhaled to keep her voice steady. "It's always a good idea to do as one's boss suggests. And there are a lot of different ways to get some rest, aren't there?"

"Och, aye. There are." He stood and before she could protest, he'd scooped her into his arms and started walking towards their bedroom.

"Is it going all manly on me, are ye?" She attempted a Scottish accent again, but it only made them laugh as he deposited her on the bed.

"Oh, lassie," he crooned as he began to undress her. "I'm only just gettin' started."

"Is there a reason you never use your photo in your reporting?" Mac asked, brushing a lock of hair from her eyes.

They'd made love twice. Once with a gasping, heated frequency, like lovers about to be separated. And then again after a cup of tea with more than a wee dram of whiskey, in a slow, almost lazily languid and fluid way as lovers will do when they have all the time in the world.

Mac only hoped the second was just a hint, maybe a promise of things to come.

"A lot of journalists don't," Anne said. Her head was pillowed against him and to Mac, nothing had ever felt so right.

"Yeah, but you're no ordinary journalist," he responded.

She turned so she could place her hands on his chest and rest her chin there. "Explain."

"I've been checking up on you again," he admitted.

"You've discovered I really can't play Ode to Joy

on the kazoo?" She batted her eyelids. "Sorry to let you down, Marine."

He laughed and his free hand stroked her back. "I've never liked the kazoo," he said. "The harmonica is more my style. But over the past four years, you've been offered jobs at major newspapers in New York City, Chicago, and San Francisco with I would guess a much higher salary than what you're making now."

"Your digging was with Stanley Harris," she accused, but her eyes twinkled like summer light. "He told you this, didn't he?"

"Yeah," Mac said. "When he told me to keep an eye on you because you'd be so determined to find Katie and the other kids, you'd be hard to handle, I asked him to tell me what he could about you. That little piece of information was the first thing he shared. Said he'd known a lot of good reporters in his career–male and female, and that you were in the top three. That when you were on a story, you were like a terrier going to ground and you wouldn't let up until you'd finished, and that he was damn glad you turned down all those offers to stay in Knoxville. My question is, why?"

"East Tennessee is my home," she said simply. "I've traveled around the world and seen wonderful things. The landscapes, the cultures, the food–don't get me talking about the food. And the people were like most people everywhere. Decent, caring folks who'd do anything to help someone else. But those places aren't home. East Tennessee is. And there you go."

She yawned and turned to nestle against him again. "Say goodnight, Mac."

Only after he was sure she was sleeping, did he dare whisper, "Good night, *mo chridhe." My heart.*

CHAPTER 19

Sunday Morning

"Stanley? It's Anne. Do you have a minute?"

She'd woken early, curled against Mac and suddenly craving coffee. He was so deeply asleep he hadn't roused even while she was in the shower. Now fully dressed, ideas bubbling in her mind, she's called the man she considered her friend as much as her employer. He would be, she was sure, at his desk after the early morning service at St. John's, the Episcopal Cathedral downtown, and a few minutes' drive from *Excelsior* and his loft apartment.

"A lot of things happened yesterday," Anne said, after savoring her first sip of coffee. "So much, I think the case will break wide open today."

"You've found the kids?" Stanley's mellow baritone jumped a half octave.

"Not yet, but we will," Anne said, praying her hopes weren't running ahead of her. "Since you're already downtown, why don't you come over to *Ramsey's* and we can talk about it? We're on the fifth floor."

"I must have known you were going to call," Stanley chuckled. "I stopped at *Sophia's* and bought a bag of croissants. I'll get a cab and be over in a few minutes. It's too cold to walk."

"It must be if you're taking a cab," Anne chuckled. Stanley's refusal to drive short distances was legendary at *Excelsior.* And since his loft apartment was blocks from the paper, he walked to work every morning. "Waste of gas and taking someone's parking space," he often said.

"I'll be waiting in the lobby for you," Anne said.

She ended the call and after returning her cup to the kitchen, headed for the closet in the living room to get out and put on her coat, making sure she had her key card in her jeans pocket. After a moment, she crept back to the bedroom and picked up the large styling brush Mac had given her between bouts of lovemaking and put it in the coat's interior pocket. The hollow center contained not only a tiny, powerful flashlight but a long, slender, and very lethal-looking knife.

"Why would I need something like this?" she'd

asked. "I have no plans to be more than a few inches away from you until this is over."

"It's a new thingee BP is giving out to people we're helping," he'd explained. "Falls under the category of 'just in case.'"

"'Thingee?'" she'd repeated, unscrewing the end and shaking the contents into her hand.

"Yeah, you know. The same group of words like 'hinky.'" He'd returned the knife and flashlight to their hiding place and put the brush on the nightstand. "We'll practice throwing the knife tomorrow if we have time. Now, where were we?"

Now, waiting by the front doors in the lobby, she thought about everything that had happened since last Monday and how the past seven days had turned her world upside down. As Hank had said last night, the case was now in the hands of the police and BP's role was over.

So where did that leave her and Mac?

She tried forcing her thoughts to the story she would write when this was all over and of the happiness the kids and their families would have when reunited.

But Mac's image kept intruding into her thoughts, making thinking of anything but him impossible. She needed to clear her head.

"If this coat and Mac's sweater don't keep me warm for a few minutes, nothing will," she muttered, pushing open the doors. "I need some cold air."

An orange and white cab was pulling up to the curb as stepped outside. Its door popped open, and she stepped up to it. "That was fast," she said. "You must be hungry."

And then someone was pulling her inside, and the door was slamming behind her. The tires' screech echoed those of the cab that had plowed into her and Henry while strong hands were jerking her arms behind her and tying her hands together while a smiling Cassie Douglas pointed a revolver at Anne's chest. "So, Ms. Hamilton," she drawled. "We meet again."

"I'm coming!" Mac shouted in answer to the pounding on the suite's front door. He rolled from the bed and grabbed his jeans and t-shirt from the floor, pulled them on, and wondered where the hell his sweater was. Grabbing his phone, he limped into the living room and yanked open the door. Stanley Harris stumbled in, his expression a mixture of terror and rage. "Harris? What the fu-"

"They've got Anne," Harris gasped. "Someone in a cab just grabbed her."

"Are you shitting me?" Mac roared. "How?"

"She wanted to discuss doing a story about the case," Harris explained, putting his bags on the coffee table. "I told her I'd come in a cab, and I saw one pulling up to the front just as mine turned the corner. She must have thought it was me."

"And the sons of bitches got her," Mac growled, entering the words *They've got Anne* into his phone and sending it to Hank. "They've never stopped watching her. Did you call the police?"

"Just now," Harris said. "But how did The Cadre know the two of you were here?"

"Because they've never stopped watching her," Mac told him, "The Cadre must have placed someone here to watch us. Holy shit."

He returned to the bedroom, took his revolver and holster from the nightstand, and hung it over his shoulder before pulling on socks and his boots. His glance at the nightstand showed both Anne's phone and the hairbrush were gone. Her scent clung to the sheets and for a second, it wasn't his knee that made Mac stumble as he realized she must be wearing his sweater. Praying he would get a chance to take it off her, he returned to the office, fired up the computer, and gratefully took the cup of coffee Stanley gave him. Hank's image lit up the screen. Mac could not remember ever seeing his boss look so angry.

"How long has Anne been gone?" was Hank's first question.

"No more than five or six minutes," Stanley

answered. "I saw her being pulled into a cab just as mine was turning the corner."

"The Cadre must have guessed we'd come back here after we stopped Pettigrew at Henry's apartment and put in an operative to watch us," Mac said bitterly. "I should have checked things out–"

"You were injured," Hank reminded him sternly. "We had no reason to believe *Ramsey's* wasn't safe. And being close to KPD was in everyone's best interest, especially Anne's. Don't go there, Mac. Now's not the time. Call Grant and get him down here."

"Already here, Mr. Patterson." Grant Miller entered with a vaguely familiar-looking man. "I have officers downstairs arresting a desk clerk for conspiracy to kidnap Ms. Hamilton. And we know–or we think we know–where they're taking her." He gestured at the African American man beside him. "Lt. MacFarlane, Hank Patterson, meet Agent Barclee Anderson of the FBI."

"FBI?" Mac could only stare. In his custom-made suit and impeccable grooming, Barclee Anderson bore no resemblance to the Barclee he and Anne had met. "Have you been involved in this from the beginning?" He wasn't sure if he was angry or relieved.

"Sorry about the subterfuge," Anderson said. "But I couldn't let anyone other than Pastor Cole– my cousin–and Miller know my cover. Not even

Brotherhood Protectors, Mr. Patterson. We've been waiting for a chance to bring down The Cadre for a long time and thanks to BP, we're going to end their work–at least on this case."

"Understood," Hank acknowledged. Do we know where Anne or the kids are?"

"At a farm outside of Maryville, in Blount County," Miller told them. "This morning when we got all the suspects together to tell them they were being charged as pedophiles and with conspiracy to transport minors across state lines for immoral purposes, Pettigrew, Mac's attacker from the other night, went bat shit crazy. Seems in addition to being hired to find Henry Cooper's ledger and put Mac and Ms. Hamilton out of commission, his job was to wait at the farm for a shipment of guns scheduled for delivery today from Chicago. He swears he knows nothing about abducted kids, especially when Anderson tells them that their charges carry the death penalty. He couldn't talk fast enough to give us the farm's location or who hired him."

"I wish it did carry the death penalty." Mac eased into the coat he'd left on the back of the chair. "Who hired Pettigrew?"

"None other than our friend Robert H. Carsen, aka Scaren Hobert," Miller said. "Ms. Hamilton was right about his name being an anagram."

"That is one damn smart woman," Anderson praised.

"It's why I hired her," Harris spoke and his voice was unsteady. "Remind me to raise her salary when we get her back."

"We practically had to promise Pettigrew we'd put him in witness protection," Miller continued. "He told us about The Cadre putting an operative here Saturday morning, with the instructions to watch Ms. Hamilton."

"Hells Bells," Harris said. "I should have told her to stay up here she didn't need to come to the lobby."

"Not your fault," Mac said. "What else, Miller?"

"Blount County's finest should be surrounding the location even as we speak," the officer said. "According to Pettigrew, Carsen is only waiting for a shipment of six or seven 'luxury items' to arrive before they're sent to Atlanta."

"Damn," Mac whispered. "It's the kids."

"We're hoping so," Miller said. "But Pettigrew also said something weird about Carsen waiting on a van delivering dogs to arrive. How do dogs figure into this mess?"

"Because The Cadre is going to move the kids in the van from the Barlett-Sims Animal Shelter that's supposed to be taking dogs to Michigan today!" Mac surged to his feet. "They'll switch the vans, and that bitch Cassie will be driving the kids to Atlanta."

"Then go get the bastards," Hank ordered. "Mac, does Anne have her phone with her?"

"I didn't see it on the nightstand in our room," Mac said, not caring what Hank thought about that statement. He'd worry about it later. "I've never known her to be without it."

"She called me from it," Harris added. "Let's hope it's in her coat pocket."

"Then we can track her." Mac withheld his sigh of relief. "And if she has that loaded hairbrush I gave her last night, Cassie Douglas, or whoever the hell she is, is going to going to learn she picked the wrong cat to fight with. Let's go."

CHAPTER 20

"I SHOULD HAVE KILLED you when I had the chance," Cassie said. "I was aiming for you and Henry, but he had to be a hero. I'd love to shoot you now and toss your body out behind your precious newspaper, but my boss wouldn't let me. I think he has special plans for you for all the trouble you've caused us."

"You drove the car that killed Henry?" Anne struggled against the rope binding her wrists. "How about the bomb in my car and that man who grabbed me on the street? Was that Tyrel Franklin? You probably killed him too and left his body in the alley and claimed to have found it." Seeing Cassie's mouth tighten, Anne knew she was right. "You're with The Cadre, aren't you? Maybe even The Cadre itself."

"You're too smart for your own damn good,"

Cassie snarled. "Henry was such a wimp about you."

"Why would you want to destroy young lives and their families?" Anne fought to keep the fury in her voice. Only by being furious could she keep her terror in check.

"Money, my dear. Pure and simple." Cassie's laugh was evil personified. "Young, fresh flesh always fetches so much. And unless my boss decides to keep you for his purposes, I'll take the greatest pleasure in killing you myself."

"Won't do you any good," Anne challenged. "Brotherhood Protectors know that Carsen is Hobert Scaren and about his involvement with The Cadre, swapping the kids for guns and money. It was all in Henry's ledger. You told us about it and knew we'd go look for it, so you sent that man there to stop us. You thought you had it all figured out, but you're screwed, Cassie. BP cracked the codes in Henry's ledger, so we've got all the proof we need–"

Cassie's slap was hard and stinging but Anne bit back her gasp. She wouldn't give the woman the pleasure of seeing her wince.

"Shut up," Cassie ordered. "Or I'll kill you right now."

Throat dry, Anne nodded. She had no desire to talk anymore. Instead, she concentrated on listening for a sound, any sound that might give her a clue to where they were going. Not that it would do her any good because the first thing Cassie had done when she pulled Anne into the taxi, was disable her phone.

But she hadn't bothered to check the inside pockets of Anne's coat where the hairbrush was stored and knowing what the brush's barrel contained, she permitted herself a tiny smile. If she could just get to it….

The ride seemed to take forever, but Anne knew it was probably not that long. Fear can be disorienting, and she concentrated on breathing as silently and deeply as possible. Her captors remained silent, and she wondered if Cassie would kill the driver and the man beside her as easily as she'd killed Henry or Tyrel Franklin. A sob rose in her throat, but she gulped it down. Mac would find her and come. After all, he was a MacFarlane and a Marine and the best damn member of Brotherhood Protectors.

And the man Anne loved. He would come.

The taxi took a hard right and then they were bumping and jostling over what must be an unpaved road. Even behind the closed windows, she could smell country autumn air, and recalling her childhood brought a small measure of relief. They jerked to a stop, and she was hauled out and dragged through a gloopy mud that oozed into her oldest, most comfortable loafers, squishing between her toes and ruining her socks.

They were in the country and at what looked to be a farm. A large van, its sides painted with images of dogs, cats, horses, and birds clatter stood in the yard. Cassie exited the cab first and took off towards a one-story house while the man from the backhauled Anne out and dragged her in the direction of the truck. A thought occurred to her and summoning up her kind of charm, she looked at him and gave him a tiny smile.

"My hands are hurting," she said, hoping she sounded scared enough. "There's no way I can fight you. Can't you untie them? They really, really hurt." From some unknown source of acting talent, tears formed in her eyes and she let them slide down her cheeks. "Please?"

"Damn, I hate when women cry," he said as the other man joined them. "Try anything and I'll cut your throat."

"Promise," Anne sobbed as he dragged her up the van's ramp. At the top, he produced his own very large and scary knife and cut Anne's bonds while his partner fitted a key into a padlock securing the truck door. Once unlocked, he shoved Anne inside and slammed the door behind her, enclosing her in darkness. The door's vibrations made her knees wobble, but Anne dug her feet against the floor. The scent of sweat and something suspiciously like a dog filled her head and she heard breathing. A lot of hard breathing. "Hello?" she called.

And then, a familiar, beloved voice asked, "Aunt Anne?

"Katie?" Anne grabbed the hairbrush from her pocket and unscrewed the bottom. "Is that you?"

"Yes," the voice sobbed, and Anne slid out the flashlight and turned it on. "It's me. It's us. We're all here."

Moving the beam around the truck's interior, Anne counted six other kids, the five missing ones and one she didn't recognize. Nancy from the shelter lay curled up in a corner, sobbing. The kids, all tied at the wrists and ankles, looked exhausted and fearful. Anne made good use of the knife to free them all and after hugging Katie first, pulled them into the best group hug ever. She stepped back and flashlight in hand, let the beam shine over them. Gail Madison with her wonderfully huge Afro. Tall, skinny Silas Horton and his size four-teen shoes. Marie Wallis is little but looks fierce in a way that would make Shakespeare proud. Eric Chan, in his ever-present Lady Vols T-shirt, now ripped and muddied. Gail Madison blinked through her beloved granny-style eyeglasses held together at the bridge with masking tape. Peter Martinez, with what had to be several weeks' worth of stubble covering his face and Anne remembered how proud he was of just having started to shave.

And they were alive. They were all alive.

But who was the girl who stayed seated in the corner, legs pulled up against her chest, arms wrapped around them? Holding out her hand, Anne said, "Hey. My name is Anne.

Before the girl could answer, Nancy's sobs rose, and she rolled onto her knees. "Will someone please tell me what's going on?" she screamed. "Are they going to kill me?"

"Nancy, hush," Anne pleaded. "You're scaring–"

"Issac called me and told me to bring the van here because there were more dogs to be transported!" Nancy's wail interrupted her. "So, I did, but some man hauled me out of the van and shoved me in here! What is going on? Are they going to kill us?"

"Nancy, I hate to be rude, but you need to shut up now," Anne ordered. "Everything is going to be alright," and thankfully, Nancy rolled into a ball again, sobbing into the floor. Giving her attention back to the silent girl, Anne asked, "What's your name, sweetie?"

"They brought her in last night," Eric offered. "Only she hasn't said a word to any of us."

"Yeah, and those pricks outside said if we started yelling, they'd kill us," Marie added with her familiar asperity. "We've been in here for hours."

"And I'm starving," Peter complained but he was grinning. Anne's arrival had restored their hope. "Are you going to get us out of here, Ms. Hamilton?"

"Honey, help is on the way," Anne assured, hoping she was speaking a future truth.

"Do our parents know where we are?" Gail asked, massaging her wrists.

"And are they mad at us?" Silas sounded like he was on the verge of tears.

"Honey, no," Anne said. "They're all planning the biggest welcome home parties ever! Burgers, pizza, wings, whatever you want. And of course, black beans and rice, veggie style for Katie!"

This brought a round of laughter and a tiny smile crossed the silent girl's features. Nancy, thankfully, had stopped crying.

"Wait." Anne faced the double doors. "Do you hear that?"

Faint but growing louder, came the sound of a siren's wail. Then another, and still another. The kids started to cheer and joined hands. Standing between Katie and Peter, Anne closed her eyes and prayed.

"Everyone in place?" Miller said into his phone.

"Yep," came the reply. "Animal transport van coming down the road. ETA 'bout three minutes."

"Move on my signal," Miller ordered. "Not until then."

They'd hidden his patrol car in a wooded area at the end of a dirt path on Carsen's property, behind an old barn. From his place in the front seat of Miller's cruiser, Mac could see a large rental-type truck as well as a van painted with the animal shelter's logo and he could swear that even at this distance, he could hear the barks and howls of excited dogs. At Miller's request, officers from the Blount County Sheriff's Department were well hidden and scoping out the roads leading to the property. No way in hell these monsters were going to get away.

"There's the van." Mac found he could do no more than whisper. "God above, it looks just like the other one."

The identical van lumbered down the muddy driveway and came to a stop beside the other. The door of the first swung open and Cassie Douglas hopped down just as Robert H. Carsen exited from the other.

"Now!" Miller commanded into his phone, hitting the accelerator. "Move now!"

The cruiser shot forward, hurtling toward the parked vehicles. Shock and disbelief kept Cassie and Carsen frozen in place for a second or two, but as they turned to run, half a dozen police cars, lights flashing and sirens wailing, zoomed up the drive, circling them and men poured out, weapons drawn. Mac was out of Miller's cruiser, revolver in hand, before it came to a stop. "Get on the ground!" he roared as Miller and Anderson followed him. "Do it now! Anne? Where are you?"

"In the truck!" He heard her scream. "We're all here!"

Two of the men from Blount County kept their guns trained on the prostrate Carsen and Cassie while others headed toward the house. Miller handed Mac a pair of bolt cutters. "I think you're going to need these. Agent Anderson? Would you like to do the honors?"

"It will be my pleasure." Anderson smiled and strode forward to address Carsen and Cassie. "Agent Barclee Anderson of the FBI. Robert H. Carsen, Cassandra Douglas, I arrest you…"

Bolt cutters in hand, Mac charged up the truck's ramp, snapped the lock, and yanked open the doors. Sunlight poured inside as six kids wobbled down the ramp, holding hands and the medics Miller had included in the rescue team led them back to the waiting ambulances. Nancy from the shelter, sobbing hysterically, crawled after them, and it took two of the medics to half drag, half carry her the rest of the way.

And then Anne was in his arms, and they stumbled down the ramp together. Mac pressed her to his chest, and he didn't know whose heart was beating faster. "Are you alright?" he whispered against her hair.

"Yes. I– wait a minute." She pulled away and ran back up the ramp and inside the large truck. "It's okay," he heard her call. "We're safe. No one is going to hurt you. I promise."

She appeared again, holding the hand of a tall, beauty of a brunette with dark eyes who looked a bit older than the others and Mac's heart dropped. For a moment he couldn't breathe and all he could do was stare at the girl. "Oh, my sweet and blessed Savoir," he gasped. "Lily?" His question was a mix of disbelief and hope. "Lily Evans?"

Eyes wide with terror, the girl pulled her hand from Anne's grasp, and she lurched back as if seeking the safety of the truck's interior.

"Lily?" Mac whispered, moving to the foot of the ramp. "It's Uncle Mac."

The girl froze, her gaze roaming over his face. After a long moment, recognition erased her terror, replacing it with a radiant, trembling smile.

"Uncle Mac?" She took a tiny step towards him and then another. "Uncle Mac?"

Anne slipped into the truck as a sobbing Mac opened his arms to enfold Lily Evans against his chest. They sank to the ramp, and Anne's heart broke with happiness for the man she loved and who had carried too much guilt for far too long. Today, hopefully, with the rescue of the kids the last remaining shards of that guilt and grief had been exorcised. As a good Marine–and probably a Brotherhood Protector too–would say, "Mission accomplished."

At last, they rose, and after scrubbing their faces with a quickly produced handkerchief from his pocket, Mac motioned for Anne to join them. As she took his hand, she knew his demons were gone. "Hi, Lily," she said. "I'm Anne and I've heard so much about you. I can't wait to meet the rest of your family."

"And you will," Mac said, sliding his arm around her waist to walk them down the ramp. "And it starts with a phone call. Then you and me–" he pointed at Anne–"need to talk to Sergeant Miller and his men before they haul away the garbage."

He took out his phone, punched the screen, and for a moment, Anne thought he would weep again. But then the man she loved was grinning. "Hey, Parker," he said. "Are you sitting down? Good. There's someone here who wants to talk to you, buddy."

He handed Lily the phone and choking back a sob, she said, "Parker? Brother? It's Lily. I'm with Uncle Mac."

She listened, and tears running down her face began to sing the old children's song, *Look There, Daddy,* about horses in pajamas and birds in tuxedos. Only she sang 'brother' instead of daddy.

"That's her," Mac sighed, holding on to Anne as if he needed her support. "That was always Lily's special song.

"How much do you think she remembers about her family?" Anne asked. "Fourteen years is a long time for a child to be gone."

"I don't know," Mac sighed. "But like the others, she has family who loves her and never stopped believing that one day she'd come home."

"And look who's coming," Anne murmured. Shackled at the wrists, Robert H. Carsen and Cassie Douglas came forward, each with a police officer on either side. Carsen was babbling about calling his lawyers, and a travesty of justice, but defiance and arrogance marked Cassie's features. Mac signaled Carsen's escorts to take him on, but for Cassie's to stop. The officers halted, waiting.

"So, Cassie," Mac drawled. "Your little act the other night deserves a nomination for an Academy Award. Best performed by a monster pretending to be human. Guess I'm old-fashioned, but I'd never considered a woman might be calling the shots for The Cadre. Somehow, that makes it seem worse."

"I got nothing to say to you or your bitch," Cassie spat. "You have no idea of what you've started."

"Maybe," Mac admitted. "But at least for now, your part in it is done. Anne, do you have anything to say?"

.   .   .

THINK," Anne said, watching Miller's fellow officers haul Carsen and Cassie off the ground and shove them into the waiting police cars, "that we should invest in a company that makes handkerchiefs. We're going to need them."

"Sounds like a plan," Mac agreed. "But right now, let's get Lily and the others back to their families. Bet you they'll bring a case of handkerchiefs with them."

CHAPTER 21

Two days later

"Outstanding as usual, my dear." Stanley Harris praised, as he, Anne, and Grant Miller sat around his desk in his neat-as-a-pin office. He held up that morning's copy of *Excelsior* with its bolded headline, BUSTED! on the front page. "I believe your story do kids put it? –has gone viral. Congratulations."

Anne's story of the rescue of the six abducted teens and the discovery of a long-missing seventh had made the front page of every major newspaper–and some not so major–in the country and even some overseas. In it, she gave full credit to the Knoxville Police and Blount County Sheriff's Departments for their relentless work and bravery, especially Sergeant Grant Miller in assisting in the teen's rescue; to *Excelsior's* staff and Stanley Harris, its editor-in-chief-for their support; to Pastor Cole for providing invaluable assistance and to the families of the teens, who never stopped believing that their children would come home, safe and sound.

She had also laid wide open the presence of The Cadre in East Tennessee, and its mission of violence and trafficking of children and teens. Sons of the Smoky Mountains–some of the arrested had supplied tons of details–was also given prominent mention, along with Robert H. Carsen's role in it. Of Cassie, Anne made no mention.

And Lily Evans was with her family. Her abduction story was long and involved, but she'd promised to share it with Anne after getting used to her family again. Fourteen years gone was a very long time and there was a lot of catching up to do.

But no mention was made of Brotherhood Protectors for their help. Hank Patterson, Mac had told her, would want it that way.

"I want to do a follow-up story in a week or so," Anne said. "But the kids need time to rest and reconnect with their families. And there's enough evidence to lock up those monsters for the rest of their lives, right Sergeant Miller?"

"That's up to the DA's office," Miller said. "But I have a feeling they're doing their own version of the happy dance. Most of the arrested have already turned on each other, hoping for lighter sentences when the cases come to trial. But given the current attitude about child sex trafficking, that's not going to happen. They'll be locked up for a very long time. And even though some of The Cadre in Knoxville got away, I have no doubt we'll be hauling them back by the end of the year."

"I hope Alan Pettigrew will be given a long sentence," Anne complained. "He was helping with the transport of guns. And he did assault Mac."

"But since he gave up Carsen and The Cadre, his attorney will probably get him a vastly reduced sentence," Miller sighed.

"I guess we should be glad for his cooperation." Then he grinned and added, "Of course, what Agent Barclee Anderson and the FBI will do is another thing altogether."

"What about Cassie Douglas?" Stanley asked. "She was the leader in all of this and behind all the attacks on Anne. I can't believe she brought Henry's dog tags to us."

"It was her way of drawing me out," Anne said. "I think she must have met Henry almost as soon as she got to Knoxville with The Cadre. When she realized how much he knew about street life, she charmed and seduced him, thinking she could draw him in. She obviously knew of Henry's ledger because she told us about it, thinking we would go find it. When he realized who and what she was, he dropped her."

"She must have had her own people watching him, thinking he'd told you what he'd learned about them," Miller said. "The Cadre knew you wrote that story about them last year. By killing you both, they hoped to continue their work in East Tennessee."

"Ironic, isn't it?" Anne said sadly. "That Henry's ledger up until the last few months only described his own PTSD, and his work in reaching out to other homeless veterans, trying to get them help. His mention of The Cadre and Cassie was brief, but I hope it's enough to keep her locked up for good."

"We owe Lt. Tyler a great deal of thanks for cracking the code Henry wrote in," Miller said. "The DA is going to love it."

The thought of Griff Tyler and his many disguises brought a smile to Anne's face. "Griff is one of a kind."

"Hey, everyone. Is this a private party or can I join?" A familiar voice broke into the conversation. Anne turned and then sighed, grateful she was seated. Otherwise, she'd be a puddle on the floor.

Lt. Keith MacFarland, stood in the doorway, wearing the dress uniform of a United States Marine, his cap tucked under one arm and Anne mentally re-wrote Jane Austen's opening declaration in *Pride and Prejudice: It is a universal truth, that men in uniform are drop dead sexy and all women find them so.*

And this man in uniform was the man Anne loved.

"I thought we'd walk to Henry's memorial service," Mac announced, coming forward. "It's a beautifully warm day and St. John's is just around the corner."

"How's the knee?" Miller asked. "That was quite a kick Pettigrew gave you."

Mac's eyes twinkled. "Och, now. Several days of rest have done wonders. Especially when you have a bonnie lass by your side to be of assistance."

"One wonders though," Stanley drawled. "Just how much *resting* was done by either party."

"Stanley!" As the other men laughed, heat scorched Anne's cheeks and she knew her face was Crimson Tide red. "I'll get you for that."

"But later," Mac said. "If we're late, we may have trouble finding a place to sit. Gentlemen, we'll see you there."

Outside, Mac put on his hat and adjusted it. "How do I look?"

"Quite breathtaking," Anne said, reaching up to adjust it. It didn't need it, but she wanted to touch him.

She took his arm, and they walked the short distance towards the cathedral in silence. After a moment, she asked, "What did you mean, we might have trouble finding a seat if we don't hurry?"

"You'll see," Mac said. "What did your father say to you when he called the other night?"

Tears pricked Anne's eyes, but she blinked them back. "That he was proud of me," she managed to say. "And that he'd been in counseling for months but hadn't had the nerve to call and tell me he was sorry."

"And what are you going to do about that?"

The voice of her beloved was gentle, and Anne smiled up at him. "Like Lily, I'm going to take my time."

"I like that answer."

They rounded the corner and Anne saw the old school buses her church owned parked beside the cathedral. As Mac escorted her into the courtyard, Anne gasped and then began to cry.

At least a hundred people waited there, many of them men and women in uniform. Still others Anne recognized from her church, among them Pastor Cole who was coming forward.

"Mac called me and suggested we invite them," he explained, gesturing at the crowd. "I learned Henry Cooper helped almost everyone here with his pension or advice or even a place to stay. This is their way of saying thanks to him, and to you, Anne, for finding those who killed him."

And then Anne was sobbing in Mac's arms, and

he knew she was letting go of her own pain, worry, and tension, some of it new, some years old. Like his own tears at finding Lily, hers were tears of cleansing and healing and hope for a new beginning. Pastor Cole quietly moved to join the others.

"Och, now," Mac said, letting his father's accent enter his voice. "It's like a red-eyed banshee you'll be lookin' if you don't stop yer cryin'."

"Sorry," she gulped, taking out a handkerchief and drying her face.

"Besides," Mac said, gathering every bit of courage he'd ever possessed. "I've no intention of marrying a red-eyed woman. I've got the MacFarlane family honor to be holdin' up, don't you know?"

She stared at him. "You want to marry me?"

"Aye. I do."

Now she was frowning, as if considering his words. "For how long?"

"Almost since I first laid eyes on ye."

"Even that first day when I was such a bitch?" Now laughter hovered around her mouth and Mac felt the crowd's anticipation.

"Well, maybe the day after that," he admitted. "I did have to give up my truck for a bit and that gave me pause. Never be separating a MacFarlane from his truck. But soon after that."

"So, even though I nearly got us killed several

times, you got your knee busted and your truck was taken away again, you still want to marry me?"

"Aye."

Now she was laughing, and he knew what was coming. "Well, why didn't you say something?"

"Because, my bonnie lass and the queen of my heart," he whispered. Under the crowd's cheers, he leaned in for what he hoped was a lifetime of kisses. "You didn't ask."

ABOUT KAREN HALL

Karen Hall is a multi-published author of contemporary and historical romance and retired mental health therapist from East Tennessee. When not writing, she enjoys cooking for friends, singing in her church choir, and beating back the weeds in the flower garden. You can read more about her at http:karenhallbooks.com

BROTHERHOOD PROTECTORS

ORIGINAL SERIES BY ELLE JAMES

Bayou Brotherhood Protectors

Remy (#1)

Gerard (#2)

Lucas (#3)

Beau (#4)

Rafael (#5)

Valentin (#6)

Landry (#7)

Simon (#8)

Maurice (#9)

Jacques (#10)

Brotherhood Protectors Yellowstone

Saving Kyla (#1)

Saving Chelsea (#2)

Saving Amanda (#3)

Saving Liliana (#4)

Saving Breely (#5)

Saving Savvie (#6)

Saving Jenna (#7)

Saving Peyton (#8)

ABOUT ELLE JAMES

ELLE JAMES also writing as MYLA JACKSON is a *New York Times* and *USA Today* Bestselling author of books including cowboys, intrigues and paranormal adventures that keep her readers on the edges of their seats. When she's not at her computer, she's traveling, snow skiing, boating, or riding her ATV, dreaming up new stories. Learn more about Elle James at www.ellejames.com

Website | Facebook | Twitter | GoodReads |
Newsletter | BookBub | Amazon

Or visit her alter ego Myla Jackson at
mylajackson.com
Website | Facebook | Twitter | Newsletter

Follow Me!
www.ellejames.com
ellejamesauthor@gmail.com

Printed in Great Britain
by Amazon

38368908R00139